To
Gord "father Leo"

Thanks for all the
Support. Enjoy the

Book.

[signature: Pete _____]

THE LAST
PROPHET

BOOK ONE: GENESIS

PETER JAMES IENGO

Order this book online at www.trafford.com
or email orders@trafford.com

Most Trafford titles are also available at major online book retailers.

Printed in the United States of America.

ISBN: 978-1-4669-3989-9 (sc)
ISBN: 978-1-4669-3988-2 (e)

Trafford rev. 06/09/2012

 www.trafford.com

North America & International
toll-free: 1 888 232 4444 (USA & Canada)
phone: 250 383 6864 ♦ fax: 812 355 4082

This book is dedicated to Priscilla, and Peter Iengo, without your love and support none of this would be possible. I thank the writers of the comic world, your work inspired this.

CHAPTER 1

IN THE BEGINNING

Snow falls on the city streets of New York, clumps of heavenly white, blanketing everything in sight. Holiday spirit surrounds the city; department stores and vendors have prepared for the coming season. One young man will experience a much different Christmas this year. A small but homely apartment on West 14 and Seventh Avenue welcomes the start of our epic tail. Christian awakes from celebrating his twenty-first birthday with his stunning beauty of a girlfriend. Jessica is rushing to place her makeup and jewelry just right, making sure not to miss her important day of classes. Christian, like all men after a night of celebration, is smiling from east to west. "Come on, babe, I don't think I'm finished celebrating," rejoices Christian. "It's not your birthday anymore, so it's time to behave, and I have a long day of classes," replies Jessica.

Christian lies back down deeply, breathing in disappointment. Jessica finishes her left earring, turning toward Christian, crawling toward him across the bed like a lion creeping toward its prey. "I'll see you for dinner tonight; I'm in the mood for Italian." Jessica kisses Christian passionately, conveying her good-bye. Jessica grabs her keys, hooping out the door, wedging her right heel on. Christian yells over, "You look like a grasshopper." The simple morning sound of coffee beans roasting and the warm, inviting smell of the beans gives Christian a blast of energy. Drinking the warm coffee, cupping the outside with both hands as if rubbing sticks together, creates a warm fire.

Christian turns his small TV on; it's a small LCD TV on top of his kitchen counter. He tunes the TV to the local news channel, grabbing his cup of coffee and sitting down at the table. He slides the blinds across his window to see the relentless snowstorm impaling the city. The streets are blanketed in snow; cars can barely travel up and down. The news is covering people around the world preparing for doomsday, the quote on quote 2012 end of civilization. What people fail to realize is that the end is coming but in a very different way than imagined. The night before on the evening of Christian's twenty-first birthday and across the Hudson at the old Brooklyn navy yards, a great unearthing accrued. The ground itself trembled; a crack grew across the yard. Light broke free from the crack, a sound of earth turning, and fire hissing could be heard for miles.

The crack and light grew until a steady beam rocketed into the sky. For the brief second, it appeared a man was propelled out of it, crashing onto the ground. The impalement of his body caused a momentary quake in the ground, leaving a massive crater underneath him.

The man awoke at the center of the crater. His body was glowing brightly as if he were standing in front of a spotlight. The figure stood tall, dressed in a red tunic; the tunic covered most of his body, including a hood pulled over his head. His legs were covered in something that would be best described as a boot, but in place of leather, the boot was stitched with a glowing silver armor. Even his chest and wrists were covered in this glowing armor. Markings appeared all over the armor like no other drawings on earth; the images depict different angels and forms of angelic writing. The writing is similar to Aramaic but a form only known to angels, a language of God if you will. The images show angels fighting; across his chest is an image of two angels; their wings spread across the sky, a blot of lighting connects their two sword to each other. Underneath them is what looks like a barren land, a red-colored desert where images of hundreds, even thousands of angels are engaged in bloody battle.

Across his back and shoulders are detailed scriptures of angelic writing. The story of his rebellion and of the holy war, the Book of Satan, for the figure before the cold night air is Lucifer himself. He has finally emerged from hell, centuries of wait for this singular moment when he could walk among the living universe once again. His eyes turned toward the city skyline; a look of pleasure filled his smile. Lucifer lunched himself into the sky, flying toward the city like a bullet.

It was as if nobody saw or heard the events of last night; the city and the world seem unaware of Lucifer. The news just carried on about the 2012 prediction. Christian had enough; turning off the TV, he grabbed his coat and left the apartment. Traveling down the street, the snow cut across his face like shards of glass. Christian made his way down the east side of Manhattan to the upper west side where he entered Saint James Cathedral. It's a beautiful church that has stood tall in the city for many decades. The outside is decorated with tall angelic statues; the doors themselves are so massive they open like the gates of a castle. The inside of the church is more impressive than the outside; the massive altar is covered with a beautiful crucifix. The crucifix hangs across the entire altar; decorated on each side is a group of angelic statues. In the middle is a statue of Mary and Joseph; the ceiling is painted with images of the archangel Michael.

Ezio notices Christian walking down the rows. Ezio is the pastor of this church; he has watched over Christian since he was a boy in the church's orphanage. Christian spent most of his life in that orphanage, basically until he went off to a religious boarding school, and then moved on his own when accepted to college. Ezio greets him joyfully, "It's good to see you,

Christian, happy birthday." Christian smiles. "I'm sorry it's a day late, I was preoccupied yesterday." Ezio and Christian walk through the halls of the rectory toward Ezio's office. "That girl keeps you on your toes, my boy, she's a real catch." "She's the best; it's why I'm marrying her," Christian replies. "I think of you walking these halls when you where just a young boy; it bothers me that we were never able to find you a family or a real home spending all those years here with us." Ezio speaks with a deep Italian accent; he spent most of his life in Rome working for the Vatican. He's an old man with dark gray hair covering his head and wrinkles across his face. Christian always wondered about the many scars across his face and body. He had seen them on his back and chest as a boy sneaking around the church at night but never thought to ask Ezio.

Christian replies, "It's okay, Father, I understood that you wanted to keep me safe. I'm grateful for all you did. I know it must not have been easy to keep me here and help send me to school." Ezio placed his hand on Christian, smiling in acknowledgment. "I had a mission from God to watch over you, Christian." "Yea, I don't know about that, Father, I guess it doesn't matter the world ends in a few weeks anyway." Ezio snaps his head at Christian like a dog to a whistle, his face looking so surprised. "Don't tell me you believe that 2012 bullshit." "I am a man of God, Christian, I believe what my faith tells me nothing more," Ezio replied.

The two continued to talk, sharing a glass of wine together, laughing of old times. "I should be going, Father, Jess will be out of school soon, and I was gonna grab a cab and get her from class. This storm is looking pretty nasty." "Just be careful, Christian, you're a new man today, and things are going to change for you." "Yea, turning twenty-one is not that big of a deal; I feel the same," replies Christian. Christian and Ezio exchange good-byes, hugging each other.

Lucifer walks the streets of the city; people walk past him, eyeing his unique and odd attire. A man bumps into him, turning around to make eye contact with Lucifer. The man feels a pain, grabbing hold of his chest; he stumbles forward. A woman comes walking over to help the man. He falls to the ground, gripping his chest; the man is having a heart attack. The woman starts to scream for help. Lucifer crosses the street, smiling under his hood. He reaches the door to an exotic nightclub; a large bouncer stands outside guarding the door. The bouncer is so pumped up you would find a picture of him next to the definition of steroids. Lucifer walks past him and is going to enter the club when the bouncer shoves him forward. "You stupid or something? It's a twenty-dollar entry fee, and you can't be wearing Halloween custom, freak." The steroids made his vocal cords sound like he was talking through a soup can. "Forgive me," Lucifer replies with a sinister smirk. The bouncer's body becomes engulfed in flames as he screams in pain. Lucifer enters the club.

The music is blasting, girls are dancing across the stage, and people are partying wildly.

Lucifer looks at the girls dancing; they all can't help but stop and look at him in an indescribable amazement. "Excuse me, bartender, I would like a glass of whiskey straight up." The bartender pours the glass of whiskey. Behind him, the owner and a group of bouncers swarm him. "I don't know what you did to Tommy outside or my dancers, but you're going to wish you never came in here, pal." This comes out of the mouth of the very out-of-date seventies-dressed owner. Two large bouncers similar to the steroid junky Tommy lunge at Lucifer. Before their fists make contact, they freeze in midair; their bodies and odd expressions are frozen in mid attack. Lucifer continues to sip his drink; people in the club run out in a panic, but the front door slams shut, trapping everyone. The bartender grabs a bat from under the counter and goes to smash it over Lucifer's head, but both he and the two frozen bouncers explode, sending flesh and blood everywhere. The owner is covered in blood, crawling across the floor toward his office. The rest of the people are trying to break the front door open. However, the dancers continue to dance on stage as if in a trance while the music continues to play. Lucifer sits down, watching the girls on stage drinking his glass of whiskey.

The owner grabs his gun from his office; he fires a shot at Lucifer. Before the bullet hits Lucifer, it transforms into a dragon, no bigger than a cat. The dragon flies through the owner's chest, ripping a hole right through him. The dragon spins around toward the screaming cries of the people trying to break the door down. The dragon unleashes a storm of fire from his mouth, burning the people alive. The girls continue to dance; the screams are soothing to Lucifer. "This place will do just fine."

Christian is struggling to navigate through the storm. Hailing a cab seems impossible as most of the streets are roofed in snow. He decides to dart down a back alley; the tall buildings are providing some cover against the snow. The alley is damp and cold. Christian covers his body tightly with his jacket; he feels funny, and a sense of uneasiness has come over him. High above him on a nearby rooftop, a figure is jumping from one building to another. His reflexes seem superhuman; the man is covered in a similar outfit to Lucifer's. Instead of red, the tunic is white, covered in the same silver armor. Patterns of black, gold, and blue material are lined across the tunic and armor. The hood covers his face as well. The man lands on the rooftop directly above the alley and Christian.

Christian notices a bum lying on the ground; the man's body is covered in a blanket. Walking past the man, a voice is heard. "Going somewhere, Prophet?" Christian stops, turning toward the man. "Excuse me?" The man stands up, removing the blanket from his body. The man clearly does not look like a bum; his body covered in similar tunic. However, his body is not covered in different patterns of material, just one piece of red across his chest. The entire tunic is jet black with similar armor covering his body.

"So this is the one, the chosen one, even now you still have no idea who you are and what is happening. You are pathetic just like the rest of your race!" Christian looks at the man in terror and confusion. "Listen, weirdo, I don't know what you're smoking, but leave me alone before I call the cops." The man grips his fists tight, closing his eye. The ground underneath Christian begins to shake. The man's body is trembling, and his arms are rising up and down in a slow motion, almost looking like they are controlling this natural force. The man begins to scream; the volume and intensity in his screams and motion are controlling the ground underneath Christian. The ground cracks into cubes underneath Christian's feet. He falls over. A piece of concrete lifts up in midair and impales him in the chest, blasting him into the side of a brick building.

Christian's back breaks the brick wall behind him. He screams out in pain as blood spits from his throat into the cold air. Christian falls to the ground, smacking his face on the hard ice. "You're so weak and pathetic. If not for who you are, that impact would have killed you. One more should do the trick." The man begins to the do the same thing he did before, gripping his fists tight. The pieces of concrete lift into the air instead of one; he sends a handful flying toward Christian. Dazed and confused, Christian stands frozen, awaiting his impending death. Before the pieces of concrete make contact, the figure from the rooftop drops down. In a flash, the figure dropped in front of Christian. The pieces of concrete are destroyed. Before hitting the strange figure, an invisible wall seemed to shield him, and as the concrete made contact with this wall, it shattered into dust, blown away by the howling wind.

The bum turned killer assassin belched in anger. "*You*! I should have known you would come to rescue him, Michael; you can't stop us this time. You're too weak, and to place the fate of all this in the hands of a human is as foolish as this crusade." The figure turns toward Christian. "You must run. It's important you make it out of here safely. I can handle this, go now!" Christian's brain could not process what was going on, but his body seemed to respond to what the man was saying, and he started running toward the street.

The bum lunches two more pieces of concrete at Christian. The figure, now known as Michael, lifts his right hand palm open toward the flying pieces and causes both them to explode in midflight. Christian ignores the noises behind him and continues to run down the street, darting around speeding cars. The bum turns toward Michael. "I don't care who you are. I'm not afraid of you." Michael smiles at the bum. He expands his right arm out; appearing in his hand in a bright flash is a glowing sword. It is a medieval-looking sword. The hilt is an iron color, the top and side patterns of the hilt are designed as a crucifix, and the blade expands out as if the bottom of the cross.

Michael expands his right arm out, forming a similar sword in his palm. His sword, however, is larger in its size, and the hilt is a bright gold. His blade is covered in angelic writing and images. The man runs toward Michael, lifting his sword above his head. He strikes his sword down at Michael's head when Michael counters the strike by colliding the two blades. On contact, the two blades spark energy across the alley, burning holes in the buildings around them, engulfing the whole alley in a bright white light. The two continue to exchange strikes; Michael is more on the defense. Every time the swords collide, sparks of energy fly all over, and a bright light engulfs them. Michael dodges his latest's thrust forward, sliding to the right. When he kicks the man in the side, the blow packs so much punch that a loud boom is heard, and the man is sent falling across the alley and into a wall. The man smashes into the wall from the impact covered in brick. Michael lifts his sword above his head, holding the hilt with his two hands; the sword begins to glow even brighter when Michael slices the sword straight down. Expanding from the blade of the sword is a slice of energy; the energy cuts throw the rumble, cutting the man in two. Seconds later, the area is covered in a massive explosion.

Christian rips the door open to his apartment. He locks the door and crabs his dresser, placing blocking his door. In a panic Christian, grabs a bottle of vodka from the freezer and pours a glass, drinking it down quickly. "It's okay, just stay calm, what you saw was a combination of poor sleep, stress, and the weather. See, that makes perfect sense." Christian takes another shot of the vodka, taking a deep breath. "You're not crazy, Christian, and it's not the weather." These words came from Michael, the man from the alley, who is now standing in Christian's living room. Christian turns in pure shock, looking over at his front door which still is locked covered by his dresser. "How . . . how did you get in here?" These words trembled out of Christian's mouth. Michael lowered his hood, revealing his face—a soft and fair face. His skin was light; his eyes were a deep shade of blue like the color of the ocean. He doesn't look much older than thirty. "I'm an angel. I can kind of pop in and out of anywhere." Christian grabs a knife from his kitchen counter, slowly walking toward the living room. "I can assure you that knife won't be needed. Allow me to introduce myself. My name is Michael." "As in the Archangel Michael, like Michael?" Christian replied in a sarcastic tone. "Yes, I'm afraid we don't have much time for this, Christian, more will come for you." Christian stands frozen in disbelief. "If you don't get your crazy ass out in the next second, I'm calling the police." Michael approaches Christian, the feeling of anxiety and fear comes over Christian's body. "I will respect your wishes but heed my warning. Lucifer and his army will come for you. You're the only one who threatens his plans, the only one capable of stopping him." With those last words, a bright flash blinds Christian like the flash of a camera, and Michael is gone.

Deeply disturbed by the events that just transpired, Christian flees his apartment, deciding to see Jessica at class. *At least, she might make sense of all this,* he thought to himself. He kept thinking it was a daydream—maybe a tumor or some trick of the storm, but the words Michael spoke felt somehow very real to him. It was hard to admit that, but it's almost like hearing a familiar song; you don't quite know the whole song, but you recognize a verse or two. Traveling through the city seemed more and more difficult between weird, super-powered bums to the relentless snow storm. The air is covered in white; it looks like the hand of God took a pastel shade of white and just brushed over everything. No matter what, Christian pushed on, racing to reach Jessica, racing really to make sense of these events and the new feelings inside him.

CHAPTER 2

THE CREED

Burned corpses of the patrons at "the Ecstasy" lay all across the carpeted floor. The multicolored diamond patterns are now stained with red blood and black ash. Lucifer is being pleasured by a few of the exotic dancers when the slight crackle of thunder is heard. It's a faint noise that accompanies an angel whenever they appear. See, angels can travel anywhere in the world; they use the elements of the heavens, clouds, and the sound waves associated with thunder to move freely from one place to another. Higher-class angels known as "archangels" can simply move around anywhere just by a mere thought.

During the holy wars when Lucifer rebelled against God, he led an army of angels who believed in his ideals. The army was referred to as "the Fallen." When Lucifer was banished to the "Lake of Fire," the fallen angels hid on earth among humans. They continued to serve Lucifer's will until the day when he would once again be free to lead them. Over the centuries, Lucifer created evil entities from the souls in hell. The demons and supernatural forces we've named over the years in fairy tales and folk law have been the rebirth of human souls. These cursed souls where transformed into demons; demons sent back to earth to communicate with the fallen angels and torture mankind.

The soldiers have now returned to their general. Mephistopheles, Aerial, Azazel, and Leviathan all bow before Lucifer. He dismisses the exotic dancers and stands in the middle of his servants. A circle is formed with Lucifer in the middle; a surge of energy blasts through all them, an electrical current connecting one around. For a few moments, the current illuminates the club. Lucifer cries out, increasing the intensity of the surge. Finally, releasing it, he says, "Feel your renewed power! For centuries you have grown weaker and weaker, living in this realm among these mortals. Now your strength has returned, rise!" Mephistopheles is a brute angel; most angels are more defined and slender in their figure but not Mephistopheles. He is tall and blocky—a Mack truck would be a good comparison. The angels are all dressed in similar attire—angelic tunic robes with a glowing silver armor across their wrists, legs, and chest. They each have a band of red material stretched across their chest and upper biceps.

"My lord, we have found the prophet. I sent Uriel to kill him, but . . . he failed." Before Mephistopheles can finish speaking, Lucifer lunges toward him, grabbing hold of his neck. "You told him to kill the boy, huh!" The loud tone in his voice shakes the very walls of the building; a chill is sent through the other angels and a feeling of fear and panic fills the room. "I'm sorry, my lord, the prophet threatens you." Lucifer drops Mephistopheles, "How did Uriel die? I can no longer sense him." Mephistopheles is rubbing his neck; giant imprints of Lucifer's fingers can be seen across his neck. "Michael, sire." Lucifer smiles, laughing to himself. "Oh, dear brother, I should have known it was you. I can smell your very presence. Michael is in the city, so you all must be careful." Mephistopheles smiles, making light of Lucifer's comment. "We can handle him." Lucifer pounds his fist against the bar. The building trembles from the force.

"Do not every underestimate him; he's more powerful then you can imagine, and he will kill the three of you idiots if he so desires; that's if I don't beat him to it! For now, your task is simple. Find the boy and bring him to me." Lucifer is running his fingers across the rim of his glass; in the center of the glass, the whiskey is displaying an image of Christian's face. "Just bring the boy to me, Mephistopheles, and quickly." Mephistopheles looks at the other angels, shaking his head in acknowledgment of the order. The sound of thunder is heard again as the angels disappear. Lucifer is left alone standing at the bar, sipping his drink. He looks into the mirror in front of him.

The mirror starts to move like waves of water; an image is displayed across it like a TV screen. He sees Christian running through the snow. "I'm afraid faith has dealt you an interesting hand today, my boy. Let's see if you're truly who I think you are!"

Christian finally arrives at the college. Ripping the doors open, he runs through the halls and down three flights of stairs. He jets through the science department and sees Jessica coming out of her class. At this point, Christian is covered in snow and frozen from head to toe. Jessica is not only shocked to see him but speechless at his appearance. "Babe, what's going on? My god, you're soaking wet and frozen. Jesus." Jessica walks him to the common area on the floor; she takes her coat off and wraps it around Christian. He's trembling. "Now, baby, tell me what's going on. You look terrified." Christian explains the events of the day; he breaks it down piece by piece as it happened. His voice is trembling throughout the whole story; you can hear the confusion and fear. Jessica grows in worry for him. She cuts him off before he can finish the story. "Just stop, you are not making any sense and worse, sounding crazy. Now just calm down and take a deep breath. What we need to do is call the police and report that you were mugged and followed back to the apartment." Jessica continues to make sense of the events in a more rational manner.

Christian starts to calm down, even believes Jessica. This logic makes way more sense that what he thought. To be honest, he even liked looking it at this way; it gave him a sense of comfort. Jessica had that ability. She always knew how to make him feel better, safe, and loved. "Listen, baby, I think you should go to the police. There's a precinct a few blocks from here, just go there; tell them what happened, and I will meet you after class, okay?" Christian nods his head in agreement; Jessica rubs his face, telling him everything's going to be okay and that she loves him. The two kiss, and Christian heads out the building. Christian has dismissed the crazy thoughts in his mind and really subscribed to Jessica's version of the story.

The warmth he experienced a few moments ago seems like a decade. The temperate and sheer force of the storm is unrivaled. *A few blocks away, safety waits,* Christian thinks to himself. He can maybe put an end to this ridiculous and weird day. A shadowy figure bolts across the street; he notices something move quickly in the corner of his eye. Christian cuts through Chambers Street and decides to go through Washington Market Park, hoping to shield himself from some of the storm and cutting into Greenwich which is a few blocks from the station. The park looks more like the North Pole blanketed in snow. The wind is howling, and an uneasy feeling has come over Christian, almost the sense that he's in danger—a bad energy in the air. He sees the dark shadow bolts by once again, but he's too slow to catch it. Dismissing it like he's done mentally with everything that happened today, he pushes on.

The howling and wind gets worse; Christian now stops. His feeling has grown worse; something is wrong. The shadowy figure now appears, walking from out of the trees and mountain of snow. "Who's there?" Christian feels stupid even yelling something so cliché. There's no response from the man walking toward him. His slow walk, combined with the cold features on his face, made Christian anxious. Christian attempts to rub his eyes and look through the thick air. The man's hand begins to glow a bright red. The man is forming energy into his palm; forming into a ball, the man aggressively fires it at Christian.

The blot of energy rockets toward him, smashing into the ground no more than a foot in front of him, propelling Christian into the air. The ground is scorched from the blast. Christian is moaning in pain, trying to get to his feet. His vision is blurred. For the moment, he is dazed and can't get up. The man continues to approach him. The man can now clearly be seen, and he is a member of the fallen "Leviathan." Leviathan grabs Christian by the hair, lifting him into the air, dangling in front of him. "You are truly pathetic. I should rip your beating heart out of your chest, but I cannot. It's time to go boy." Before Leviathan can teleport out of the park, an arrow smashes into his arm. He drops Christian. The arrow sends an electrical current through his body similar to a tazer. Not very effective against an angel but good enough to buy some time.

A group of four men jump out from the bushes and trees. They run to Christian's aid. The men are dressed in similar attire to the angels but with many differences. Their tunic robes are not strapped with the glowing armor or angelic writings and images. They also have many weapons attached to them. Two of the men are ordered to grab Christian and pull him back from the fight. Two other men in the group engage Leviathan. Leviathan addresses the group of men as "the Creed" and the two men as Markious and Anthony. Anthony engages Leviathan by unsheathing his sword and lunging toward him. Leviathan catches the blade of the sword with his hand. He pulls Anthony toward him and smacks Anthony across the face; the force of his blow sends Anthony flying across the park.

Markious grabs his bow and fires a few arrows at Leviathan. Leviathan forms a shield of energy in front of his body; each arrow shatters on impact. Markious grabs a large dragger from the side of his leg, flipping into the air in a downward motion to stab Leviathan. Leviathan stops him in midair, freezing him. He then takes both of his hands as to push a blast of energy onto him, and the blast crashes him into a nearby tree. Christian looks at the two guys, now dragging him away from the fight. "Who are you?" "Aww," he speaks, "I'm Joseph. This is my brother, Christopher." "We're here to help," replies Christopher. Christopher is a simple-looking man; he has clear and defined Irish features—freckles dotted across his cheeks and an autumn shade of hair.

Christian looks over to Christopher. "Are those two guys going to be okay?" Joseph gives a concerned look to Christopher. "I'm not sure; we've never encountered something as powerful as Leviathan. Demons, yes, but a fallen, no." Christian takes a deep breath; a smell feels the air similar to burnet tare. It reeks. More importantly, Christian thinks to himself why people haven't come running over to their aid, and what happened to the police. Surely sounds of explosions would alert New York's finest. "I think you two should help them. I mean I'm praying the men in black show up soon to erase my memory, but until then, I think your friends need your help." Joseph responses by telling Christopher he will stay with Christian. So Christopher jumps into battle to aid Markious and Anthony.

Joseph shares similar features to Christopher; you can tell he comes from an area in Ireland or Scotland. Although his exterior is more rugged then Christopher's, his face is covered in a light bread, and his hair is a black as the night sky. Anthony is engaged in sword play with Leviathan. There blades are colliding, causing a wave of sheer energy to propel from the sides of the blade. The impact of their strikes can be felt all around them; even the sound crackles like an electrical hum. "Impressive. I see Michael blessed you with an angelic blade, but you're still only a man!" Leviathan charges his blade; it begins to glow brightly when it makes contact with Anthony. It is true that Anthony is only a man, and his blade has limits. The strike is too powerful. Anthony's blade flies out of his hand and across the park, and Anthony is blasted through the snow. The force is so great Anthony propels backward; his feet cut through the ground underneath him like a rake cutting through grass. Markious fires an arrow quickly; the arrow makes contact with Leviathan face.

It shatters on impact; the attack had no effect on Leviathan. "You fools won't learn, will you? The boy is coming with me!" Leviathan grips his fist tight; his entire body begins to glow brightly. Unaware of the impending attack, Christopher smashes his sais deeply in Leviathan's back. The blade does not pierce his skin, but it does knock Leviathan to the ground. This gives Markious the time to help Anthony recover and rejoin the fight. "So, Joseph, right? While we are in the Twilight Zone, I figure I might as well ask some questions before we're all ripped to pieces." Joseph looks very confused at Christian's humor. Before Christian can ask the many questions blogging his mind, Anthony, Markious, and Christopher come hurling at them.

They all fly to ground like a ton of bricks. Joseph jumps in front of Christian, armed with his wooden staff. Fear runs through Christian's body. His mind is racing. Thoughts of Jessica entire his mind. He can't help but think of her, how much he misses her, and if anything happened to him, how he wouldn't be able to hold her one more time. The thoughts become more intense as does his panic. His mind is now running so fast the terror takes over, and his body goes autopilot. Joseph can hear Christian grunting behind him. His grunting grows louder and louder. Everyone is now focused on Christian; his body is shaking. Gripping hold of his fists, holding them so tightly, blood is oozing from his hands. The ground begins to crack apart underneath him; lines break across all the way to Leviathan feet. Christian can no longer contain his feelings and emotions; he releases a howling cry. His screams rattling the very park itself, and a wave of energy propels from his body, breaking apart the ground underneath him. The debris smashes into Leviathan.

A massive cloud of energy is circling Christian, almost like a living form circling and turning around his body. His eyes are flared in rage, and his teeth are grinding together. Sounds of police sirens can be heard in the distance, and people are now flocking to the park, looking in amazement, but the storm makes it impossible to clearly see. Leviathan flies toward Christian in a fit of rage, but the energy circling Christian acts as an unbreakable wall. Leviathan hits the energy; it cuts through his body like a blade. Leviathan jumps back, grabbing and holding his shoulder, now oozing blood. He forms a ball of energy in his left hand and fires a blast of energy at the circling shield around Christian. The beam of energy connects with the shield; an explosive sound is heard for miles. The sound cracks the windows of cars parked all across Chambers Street.

Leviathan is struggling to hold the beam of energy; he pushes against the shield, channeling more of his power into the intensity of the blast, hoping to rip through the shield. Christian continues to stand still in the center; his expression is very cold and lifeless. Anthony yells over to Markious, "We are too exposed, and the police are growing near. We must go." Markious looks completely confused. "And how would you like me to do that?" Christian looks over at Markious. Markious hopes Christian can understand him; he makes a nod and hand motion to point attention to the growing crowd outside and police sirens. Christian understands; he flares his arms in a forward motion as if commanding the circular energy to blast forward. Leviathan is overpowered; he is engulfed and blasted into pure dust blowing away.

For a moment, everyone is in a state of shock and is silent. Christian passes out, falling to the ground. Anthony runs over to check on him. "He's alive, just out of it." Markious can see the police storming the park. "That's great, but we're out of time. We need to move, *now*!" Anthony lifts Christian. The five men dart across the park and away from the police. Anthony turns to Markious, saying, "We must head toward the church and see Ezio."

Lucifer is perched on a rooftop, peering into the city. "They're so full of sin, Father, all of that you have given them, they use to gain power and rule over one another. They're stained in the blood of sin. I warned you of this, and instead of trusting me, you cursed me to that prison. It's time these monkeys learned their place. I will prove my true loyalty to you." Lucifer snaps his fingers together; the force of the snap sounds like steel drums colliding. The sound echoes across the rooftop and down the city streets. Just like that, the sound is gone; black mist emerges behind Lucifer. It swirls around, forming two figures. They're horrific in sight with sinister-looking eyes. Tall, around eight feet, their skin is cracked and rough like a reptile. Areas are covered in spots of hair.

Their faces are villainous with red—and yellow-colored eyes and goblinlike features. Razor-sharp drooling teeth, the demons are standing before Lucifer, snarling, awaiting orders from their master. "I can see into his mind and feel his doubt. It's possible the fallen might fail. So we need to motivate our little hero. You two will go to the college, find the girl, and let the boy come to you. Whatever you do, do not kill him or her. She will cloud his judgment; human emotions make them weak." The two demons morph their bodies into regular-looking men, wearing black coats.

Christian is dreaming he's in New York City, but a very different New York. The city is consumed in a blaze of fire; buildings are burning around him. Christian is walking through Times Square, flabbergasted by the burning city. He can hear people screaming in the distance, and the far-off sounds of emergency vehicles. A figure is standing in the middle of the square; Christian continues to approach him. A sharp pain comes over him. He grabs his forehead; images flash. He sees Jessica screaming, running for her life down the street while the two demons cash after her. Christian can feel her terror. He awakes to find himself lying down in a strange bed. Startled and alarmed by the dream, he runs out of the room. Something is oddly familiar about this place.

He realizes why this place seems so familiar; Ezio is standing in front of him, talking to the four men encountered in the park. Christian stumbles over, still a little dazed. Ezio quickly assists him in grabbing his balance. "Easy, Christian, you should continue to rest." Christian backs off from the group of men; Anthony approaches him. "Please, Christian, I promise you we mean you no harm. Our goal was to keep you safe and protect you back at the park." Christian takes a sip of water from a nearby glass Ezio poured him. "Funny way of showing it, I had hoped this was some horrible dream or bad Thai food reaction. How did they drag you into this, Ezio? I mean, are we hostages or something?" Ezio rubs his face in an anxious manner. "No, Christian, I invited them here to keep you safe, to explain everything; see I know the Creed for many years."

Christian is startled. "What are you talking about? How could you know them? Somebody needs to explain to me what's going on right now, or I'm marching to the police like I intended." Markious, clearly the impatient type, grabs his knife; and in a deep Irish accent, addresses Anthony. "This is useless. We have demons to kill, and I'm itching for a fight." Christian is really blown back from that comment "Didn't we just come from a fight? What's his problem?" Anthony motions for Markious to sit down and relax. "Christian, I would like to finally explain everything to you, who you are, and more importantly, who we are, and what's going on." Christian is perplexed what to do, but at this point, his curiosity has gotten the best of him, and it's been a weird day.

Anthony sits down next to him; the setting seems to warrant the coming of a long tale. "We've been around for a very old time. See, long ago, I was a general in the Christian Crusade. At that time, I thought I was doing God's work. I realized too late the sins I committed and the lie I led. The worst part of it all was my wife, and children were murdered by another legion of the crusade. We had armies all over under different commands. We were all savages, poorly led and organized. I sought revenge for the men who killed my family; my sin never ended. Finally, I decided to rebel against the very cause I fought my entire life for. I went into hiding. I found myself deep inside a cave, trying to escape the harsh winter." Christian can see the images of Anthony's story in his head like a dream. Was Anthony's story this vivid, or was Christian sharing his memories.

He could see him shaking in a corner of the cave, a fire fading away in the middle of the floor. The sound of thunder rattling the very walls of the cave, Anthony continues to tell his tale. "I felt myself dying; then the strangest thing happened. I was standing on the cliff of a mountain. The air was so clean I could smell the ocean beneath me and the warmth of the sun on my face, even my illness had faded." Christian himself could see the grassy cliff, the warm sun, and the smell of the salty sea air. It was like watching a movie playing before him. "A figure appeared before me. He introduced himself as the Archangel Michael, and I figured I had died at that point." Christian can see the two speaking. "I know I've sin, the things I've done, and I know where my judgment lies." Michael pats Anthony on the shoulder. "What if rather than the punishment you seek, I offer you redemption?" Anthony is clearly confused by Michael's question. "Anthony, what if I told you that centuries from now, man would face its darkest hour. See, my brother Lucifer will be free to unleash his fury on this world in the earth year of 2012. He will obliterate the entire human race."

"How could God allow this, Michael," replies Anthony. "A young man will turn twenty-one, the month of his ascension. This boy will be a new prophet to the world, and he will possess the abilities to defeat

Lucifer." "I don't understand why you are telling me this?" Michael waves his hand across a stone; four weapons materialize on the stone. "The prophet will need someone to train him and guide him in this quest. Even know, Lucifer prays on the living with his demons; people need saving. I offer you a chance to redeem yourself. Take this creed. You will be immortal and will have the weapons and abilities to help man." Anthony walks over to the weapons brightly glowing on the stone. He sees a two sais, a staff, a dagger, and sword. "Your mission above all will be to seek the prophet out when the time comes and help him fulfill his destiny. Until then, take these weapons and find three other men as worthy to join your creed. You each will be honoring this code to never take a human life, to protect mankind from the forces of darkness, and to serve the prophet." Anthony accepts the offer, pledging himself to Michael. His body starts to glow. His body became dressed in a full white tunic, covering him from head to toe. Leather arm bands cover his wrists. Leather straps cover his legs, and a leather belt covers his waist. His new sword is strapped behind him, hanging on his back.

"After this, Christian, I had to now find the other men to serve with me to form the Creed. I served in the war with a great man; I learned he had died shortly after I learned of my own wife's death. I knew though he had a son in Ireland. When I learned his mother had died from illness, and Markious was arrested for

rebellion and to be hung. I knew I had to rescue him."
Again, Christian can visualize what's being told before
him. Anthony sneaks around the prison. He launches
an arrow at the guard on the roof. The arrow has a dull
head, and it just knocks the guard out. This alerts the
guard in front of the prison who now has run up to the
check on him. Anthony quickly darts across, entering
the prison. Covertly checking each corner for guards,
he sees two more guards at the end of the stairs in front
of Markious cell.

Anthony runs toward them. He springs off the side
of the wall, flipping over their heads. Before landing
behind them, he grabs both of their heads, knocking
them together. When he lands, the two guards fall
to the ground unconscious. "That was when I found
Markious. I knew I could trust him. His father was a
good friend and great warrior. He stood for the same
ideal and values what his father did, and I knew he was
searching for a similar purpose and redemption.

The jail reeked of human feces. Anthony made his
way to the cell containing Markious. He was badly
beaten. His clothes all torn soaked in blood. He was
shacking in the corner of the cell when Anthony
approached him. "Markious Atalis, I am a friend of your
father. I come in peace." Markious was so astounded.
He dashed forward, grabbing hold of the bars. He
looked on Anthony with a desperate and hopeful gaze;
you could see that his spirits were beaten. The guards
had clearly tortured and abused him physically and

mentally. In a swift motion, Anthony slashed the bars open; his sword cut through the iron bars like Jello. Markious was stupefied and unsure what to do; his trust had been weighted down in the last few months, but something seemed right about Anthony. Before he fell to the ground in pure exhaustion, Anthony grabbed hold.

Markious finally awoke a few days later. He found his wounds mended, and he was dressed in new clothes. He was lying in a comfortable bed in a beautiful villa facing the water. He could see Anthony talking to what looked like a young monk. The man bowed his head "at once," exiting the balcony. Anthony turned, looking out onto the water. Markious reached for his sword lying on a table in the middle of the room. Anthony says, "I wouldn't do that, my friend. The sword has a habit of injuring anyone's touch but my own. The danger you feel is not present here. Put your mind to ease and join me." Markious walks out onto the balcony; he can smell the salt from the sea and the many fragrances of the garden beneath him. Many nuns are attending to the garden; its many flowers make for a beautiful pattern touching the tip of the ocean. "Why did you rescue me?" The question added a certain thickness and tension; Anthony looked fine and calm, staring across the vast ocean. "I merely fixed a wrong into a right. See, I served with your father in the war." Markious's face looked very unsettling on the mention of war. "Don't worry; I have no love for the crusades. My family was murdered while I was away. I wanted nothing but vengeance. I sought out the men responsible and killed them. I turned my back on my ways, all I knew, and looked to take my own life."

Markious was confused to why Anthony was telling him all this, more confused why he was there. "What does any of this have to do with me, or why you brought me here?" Anthony walked backed into the villa, grabbing the dragger given to him by Michael; it was one of the four blessed weapons. "You see, I had taken shelter in cave to escape a violent storm. I figured illness, or the storm would kill me. As I felt myself slip away, I awoke on top of a hill. It was majestic—no storm, the sun felt so bright and warm. The ocean was so clear; even the air seemed so calm and enchanting. A man approached me. He was the Archangel Michael. He offered me a chance to free my soul, redeem myself. He told me in the year 2012, a boy would be chosen by God to fight Lucifer and his army. This battle would determine the fate of mankind. He offered me immortality and special abilities to protect man from the forces of darkness until the year 2012. When my true destiny would be to help protect and stand with the prophet in the ending battle."

Markious, at this point, is looking at Anthony like he has ten heads or mentally ill. "Just stop. An angel gave you magical powers to live forever so you can babysit someone in the future?" Anthony smiled. "I suppose so, and there are many evil forces at work now that could use our help." Markious gazed across the garden and water. The waves seem so calm, so peaceful; he takes a very deep breath. "Anthony, even if I believed your fairy tale, what do you want from me?" Anthony walked back on the balcony and placed the dragger on the side of Markious. "I was given four weapons; one of my own. I was told to find three men—three worthy men to serve in this creed with me. Your father was a good friend and a great warrior. I know you seek purpose, and to help people, I offer you now that purpose."

Markious goes to grab the dragger. "But hear my warning, Markious, only grab the weapon if you're true to yourself, if you accept this with all your heart and truly believe; if not, it will destroy you." Markious hesitates to grab the dagger. "I have never been much for faith; I just knew what was right and wrong. People deserve that kind of justice, that type of protection." Anthony places his hand on Markious shoulder; the gentle touch puts a level of ease over Markious. "We must find God in our own way. All I ask is you stand by me and the mission." With those final words, Markious grabs the dagger, his fingers wrap tightly around the handle. He can feel the thick leather wrapping around the cold steel. The dragger makes a smooth and familiar sound sliding out. His body becomes engulfed in a bright glow. Markious has now transformed into a member of the Creed. His body is covered in the same clothing as Anthony. A white and red tunic, leather strappings across his wrists, legs, and waist. His muscles and physical appearance have even changed; his body has taken more of an athletic and toned shape.

"I feel so different, stronger, more focused somehow." Anthony smiles. "It's the new powers you've inherited. Your clothing will protect you during battle, and you now have the strength of ten men and the reflexes and senses of a jaguar. If only we could find two more good men." Markious is jumping around, slicing his dragger, testing his new abilities. "I may have a solution to that problem. I know two brothers, and well, they're not blood, but they've taken care of one another forever. There is a little odd, but you won't find better men. An added bonus, they're both excellent blacksmiths." Anthony continues to describe the setting in articulate detail. Christian still can visually see the story unfold as if watching a movie in 3D. Joseph and Christopher had fought with Markious in the rebellion; the two had left Ireland before authorities caught them. They escaped with their sister. Markious and Anthony had tracked them down to Germany. They tracked them down to a small town outside Berlin.

Christian can see the small tavern Markious and Anthony enter. The place was filled with wild drunks; people were carrying on in a jolly spirit. Joseph and Christopher were among those drunks. Christopher was arm wrestling a man twice his size. Markious and Anthony walk to the bar, ordering two pints of ale and surveying the bar. Markious takes a sip of his drink, singling in Christopher's direction. "Tell me it's not the baboon arm wrestling the giant." Anthony said this with great disappointment. "I promise he's a good man." Christopher knocks his beer over the giants head, grabbing the money from the table; the man flips the table over, yelling a loud unpleasant grunt. Joseph comes stumbling out of a room on the second floor. A naked woman is screaming at him from the room. Joseph flips over the banister, crashing onto the table.

Christopher looks down at Joseph. "I see you were a smashing hit with the red head." Joseph sees the stunned mob of giants. Their snarling look is not comforting. The mob looks like a pack of hungry wolves. "Looks like you're having the same luck; perhaps we should go." Christopher agrees with Joseph, but the man grabs Joseph, throwing him into the bar. He hurdles straight into the counter of bottles, all smashing against his back. Christopher leaps forward, punching the large brut. The punch did nothing but anger the man. Before the punch makes contact with Christopher's face, Anthony grabs the man's fist. Markious helped Joseph to his feet. Anthony addressed the man calmly, hoping to defuse the situation. "Violence is never the answer, my friend, I would be happy to pay you the money this man owes you and send you on your way." The man begins to burst in a full-body chuckle. Joseph looks at Markious. "Markious! Jesus, Mary, and Joseph. It's been a long time. I don't think your friend is going to be okay." The man lunches a punch straight for Anthony's face.

Anthony, in one smooth and quick motion, dodges the blow by sliding to the right and knees the man dead center into his chest.

The blow packs so much force that the man falls to his knees, grabbing his chest in blinding pain. "I did not wish to get physical. As promised, here is the money the man owes you. It is rightfully yours." Anthony grabs Christopher, walking out of the bar with Markious and Joseph. Joseph, at this point, is leaning against Markious, cut all over from the glass bottles that smashed all over his body. Christopher expresses his confusion. "What just happened in there, huh? Markious, we haven't seen you in years. Now you show up in some weird monk outfit, and why the fuck did you pay that bastard?" Snow is falling outside the tavern. "I did the just thing. You stole from him, but his violence was also a sin, neither would have been a solution." Markious removed his hood, uncovering his face. "Guys, I realize this is a shock. Trust me, I haven't been vacationing. I've been in jail waiting to be hung for my crimes until Anthony came for me."

Anthony and Markious share bits of the story of everything that has happened. A look of amazement and utter shock fills Christopher and Joseph's expression. "So you're immortal soldiers for God, and you would like us to join you down the road of insanity? Clearly, that prison changed you, Markious." Markious expands his arm out, holding Christopher. "I'm dead serious, you owe me, both of you do, so hear me out!" Joseph limps over. "Chris, he's right. This is Markious we're talking about. Granted it sounds ridiculous, but what your friend did inside to that guy was pretty amazing." Anthony takes them miles away deep into the woods. The snow has stopped falling. The giant pine trees are blocking the flakes from falling; Anthony places the weapons on the stone. Now left is a wooden staff and a two sais.

Anthony looks over at the two men. "I trust Markious. I may not know you, and you, but destiny waits for no one. I need more than just soldiers, more than just followers; I need a family, a brotherhood. Markious told me you all fought once for the freedom and rights of the oppressed. You sought any fight as long as you could help good people. Give God your faith, give him your pledge, and take hold of these weapons if you truly believe in this quest in truly helping mankind."

They both take a deep breath, making eye contact with each other. Joseph shrugs his shoulder. "Oh, what the fuck!" The two grab the weapons, each are engulfed with a glowing light. As the light fades, their bodies are redefined with more muscular definition and dressed with the same white and red tunics with leather strapping's. The strapping's cover their wrists, legs, and waist. All four now stand together, forming the Creed.

Anthony finishes the story, and the vision fades like a ripple in a wave. Christian is now at the church. The story was so vivid; it was as if he was reliving every part of it. "That's how we became the Creed. We have been protecting man for generations, waiting for the time when you would be ready. Our time has come, and we are here to serve you in this final battle." Those words weighted heavily on Christian. His mind was racing in a thousand different directions; the worst part was a feeling of certainty. He connected with the story—not sure how, but he knew somehow that this wasn't all some joke. The thought crossed his mind that he might be losing his mind, developing some form of split personality disorder.

Christian looked over at Ezio, his expression somber. "Did you know about all this?" Ezio takes a deep breath. "Christian, I . . ." "Just answer my question, Ezio. Have you known my entire life?" Ezio takes an even deeper breath, rubbing his face nervously. "I was a member of an order that Anthony started centuries ago, a secret group working under the church to assist them. My mentor and good friend, Cardinal Firenze, had passed on. He entrusted me with looking after you until this day came." Christian felt angry and betrayed by Ezio. His whole life was a lie. "You lied to me, Ezio. I looked at you as a father. I trusted you. Tell me something. Did any family really not want me or was it this orders doing?" Anthony jumped into the conversation. "Christian, what we did, including Ezio, was only to protect you. The fallen and Lucifer himself would stop at nothing to kill you. We needed to keep you safe, and this was the only way."

Christian says, "Oh, I see so depriving me of a real life, a loving family, and a sense of purpose, and acceptance that wasn't important." Ezio reached over to comfort Christian, but Christian withdrew. "Don't!" A trust has been broken; more importantly, this moment has changed his life. Is he some survivor to mankind? Could this be real? Many internal questions filled his mind.

For a moment, his mind flashed the same images from his dream. They hit him like a ton of bricks. Jessica is running; her heart is pounding, and two figures are running after her.

Anthony asked, "Christian, are you all right?" "It's nothing. I just had this dream last night of Jessica. I keep seeing her running, and somebody is chasing her, but it's just a dream." "It's not a dream, Christian, it's a vision. You can feel the energy of the people around you, the people you're connected to, and she's in danger." Christian is startled. "My god, I've been so consumed with myself. If anything happens to her, I got to go!" "We will aid you, come on."

In Christian's dream, he saw Jessica running a few blocks from the college campus. They turn down west Fiftieth Street headed toward Sixth Avenue. Jessica walks out of her last class; the city is dark and cold. The blizzard is still devastating the city. The cold chill of the wind and ice rattles Jessica. She grips her wool coat tight, covering her chest. She tries to hail a cab, but in this weather, it's hard for any cars to be on the road. Standing out in that storm is equally impossible; Jessica starts to walk down the block to the subway station.

Two men start to follow behind her. They're dressed in a black pea coat and black ski hat. Jessica notices the men growing closer to her. She quickly turns around, and the two men are gone. It's as if they vanished in thin air. Turning back around, headed down West Street, the two men reappear behind her, now closer. Jessica is now alarmed; a feeling of panic comes over her. The men corner Jessica. She tries to maneuver around them, but the men keep shuffling side to side to block her attempts. Christian and the Creed just turned right on Spring Street, now headed for West Street.

Christian can see Jessica being thrown around by the two men; she's being tossed back and forth like a pong ball. She takes mace out of her pocketbook, spraying the two men. They laugh as she sprays their faces. Their eyes glow a bright red, their mouths exposing sharp teeth, drooling, and snarling. These are no men but demons inhabiting a human form. Jessica screams in terror. Christian is now closing in. One of the demons go to grab her around the neck. Before the demon makes contact, Christian tackles him from the side. The demon falls to the ground. Anthony slices his sword at the other demon, cutting his right arm off.

The demon jumps back, snarling in pain. His arm falls to the ground, burning away into ash.

Jessica jumps in Christian's arms. "What the hell is going on, baby?" "I promise you I will explain everything, but for now, let's get out of here. It's not safe." As confused as she is, especially to see these four dressed men in holy tunics, wielding medieval weapons, she trust Christian. The two demons place their hands together, combining their bodies into one. Their form has changed now to a large grizzly beast. Their body is covered in a razor-sharp gray hair, eyes the color of the morning sun. Large piercing claws, they have transformed into an animal-like creature.

Jessica shrieks in terror while Christian holds her tight. Anthony yells out, "He's a shape shifter, and more importantly, a black dog. Keep steady!" A black dog is a common creature in British folk law. Anthony slices his sword at the demon; the demon smacks his hand out of the way, roaring in protest. Markious lunches an arrow from his bow at the demon; his arrow is fashioned with a special tip. The tip is made from the bones of the dead; the bones of the deceased are powerful weapons against a demon. Not enough to kill them, but it packs a hell of a punch. The demon grabs the arrow before it makes contact, cracking it in half. Joseph and Christopher have used this time to climb the wall behind the demon, leaping it off and smashing onto its back. Joseph smashes his staff across the demons head. Startled by the hit, the demon now stumbles forward.

Christopher slices deeply in the demons back with his two sais. Blood oozes out from his open wounds. The demon bellows out in pain. Markious now lunches an arrow straight into his chest; the arrow rips into its skin like Styrofoam. The beast hits the pavement; the dark city alley has turned into a battleground. Amazingly, the storm has provided a good backdrop to muffle out the weird sounds and images from people passing by. The demon starts to attack in a fit of rage; Anthony dodges his strikes, flipping over his head, landing behind him, slicing his sword across his torso.

The demon stands in shock; his body slides apart into two pieces. Anthony has ended the confrontation, cutting the demon in half. The two halves hit the snow-covered ground, burning away in a blaze, turning to ash, melting the snow beneath it. Christian says, "So that wasn't a bit weird. I am seriously waiting for this dream to be over." Christian realizes Jessica has passed out from shock.

CHAPTER 3

DESTINY

The city is in a blaze. The colossal skyscrapers are engulfed in flames. New York City is burning around Christian. The very foundations are crumpling, and debris is falling to the streets. Similar to his last dream, Christian is back in the destroyed city walking through Times Square. This time, the figure is no longer so far from his vision but walking straight for him. The two meet in the center of the square. Christian engages the figure who visibly is Lucifer, "It's you, isn't it? I mean you're him, Satan, the devil, or whatever?" "I have gone by many names, but as you humans would call it, my birth name is Lucifer, the rest is manmade fantasy. I'm not horn-headed with a pointy tale. I'm an angel. I'm not as bad as you think," replied Lucifer.

"Is this the part, Lucifer, where you tell me you're one of the good guys, and all the bad is really for the greater good and justifies-the-means-type deal?" Lucifer smiles while observing the destruction around him with a certain pride. "No, what I will tell you is the truth—the truth that there must be a balance of good and evil. See, I provide that needed force. What you don't understand is that I was the first; I came before Michael or any other angel. I was there at the beginning when this entire universe was crafted." "What are you talking about?" interjected Christian. Lucifer delivered back with a clever smirk.

"You ever wonder how good and evil came about? I don't mean some metaphorical ideal. I mean actual good and evil; see that was here even before me. My father sent me on a mission before your concept of linear time began. I was alone, sent to a dark place between the worlds. There I found things that you or I could not imagine. That was the first time I was introduced to evil! I was given the means to lock this world, its evil away for forever or so I thought. See, when my father crafted the design for mankind, I saw something, something I had never seen since that day. It was evil, the very thing he had me locked away."

"You're talking about evil as if it were a living thing," Christian remarked. "Oh, Christian, there is so much you need to learn. Evil is something far worse than that, and it has nothing to do with me. I saw my father willing to allow that evil to break free, and I knew it was my job as it once was to stop it. That is why your race must be destroyed, or else things far worse than me will come for all of us." Buildings continued to crumble around him; the sounds of people crying out can be heard in the far distance. A feeling of sorrow and utter pain comes over Christian; his heart aches. "So you're telling me killing all of us is the only way to save the universe." Lucifer replied to his question, "As you would say, it's for the greater good. My father will understand this is the only way to keep the balance in order. You can join me, and together we can do make this right."

"You know, I honestly don't know much about this stuff. I mean I may have grown up in a church, but I'm not really interested in saving the entire human race. The only thing I'm interested in is keeping the people I love safe. Jessica is my entire life, and she happens to be one of the people in the human race you want to exterminate, so if I need to put on a funny suit and subscribe to this weird acid trip, then that's fine because I will do anything to keep her safe, including stopping you!" Lucifer is angered by Christian's words. His expression turns; a dark look is visible. He quickly appears in front of Christian as if teleporting in a blink of an eye. Lucifer grabs hold of his neck tightly. Christian reaches for his neck, choking in pain. "Listen carefully, my dear boy, I will destroy this world. You know nothing in your heart of this, you can't begin to imagine the abilities inside of you, but you're too human to understand any of it. Just stay out of my *way*!"

Lucifer lunches him across the square. Christian smashes into a parked car. The impact awakes him from his dream. Sweat is pouring from his forehand. The pounding of his heart echoes in his chest cavity. Ezio sits down next to him on the bed; Christian is startled but relieved to be out of his dream. The smell of fire and sounds of screaming people still fill his head. The dream was so real and vivid. The haunting image of the city is burned in his mind.

"Where's Jessica?" Ezio points across the room. Jessica is lying on the bed. "She's been asleep the whole time. You yourself have been out for some time." Christian is surprised to hear that. "Really how long, I remember coming here with the Creed. I was so scared, scared for myself, but more importantly, for Jessica. I guess I must have just gone out for all of it." Ezio clears his throat, trying to form his next sentence, but clearly, you can tell the words are difficult for him. "I . . . a, never meant to hurt you. I want you to know it may have started as a mission, but as soon as I met you, it became more. I loved you always and will always like a son; and as a priest, that's something I shouldn't say." Christian quickly interrupts him, "Ezio! I know, I know. I understand what you did and more importantly why you did it. I love you as a father, and nothing will change that. Truth is, instead of rejecting all this, I'm starting to believe it. That sounds completely insane, but I really am. I saw him, Ezio, I saw Lucifer in my dream."

Ezio is troubled by this. "What did he say?" Christian walks over to Jessica, rubbing her face every so gently and affectingly. He takes a cloth from the table beside the bed, dipping it in a bowl of water beside the bed. He rubs her forehand with the cool water. Jessica awakes slowly from the gentle and soothing touch. "He told me that he was doing this for the greater good. That man would bring forth the evil, real evil or some shit; the point is he's determined to annihilate us all." Jessica focuses her eyes on Christian. "You're not going to believe the crazy dream I had." Jessica realizes that she's not in her apartment but instead on a small fold out bed in a room filled with religious items.

"Oh my god, it wasn't a dream, was it? Where am I?" Jessica sprung out of bed in a panic, pacing back and forth. "Babe, I can explain, just calm down, please, just calm down." Jessica is trembling from anxiety, her chest feels tight, the walls feel as if their caving in, becoming smaller and smaller. She feels as if the air is escaping her lunges. Her mind is running wild like a runaway train. Her pacing and panic grows in its intensity. Christian grabs hold of her. In a flash, her mind returns to him. As if breaking through a glass window, shuttering the fear, the panic away. "Baby, I'm here, just relax, and please sit down. I promise I will at least try to explain what's going on." In a clear fog, she sits down on the bed. Christian sits beside her. He begins to explain everything, dating back from the events of yesterday, trying to make sense of it all. Jessica sits and listens, never interrupting him, just listening. Regardless how fantastic and implausible, she just listened.

The odd thing is the story makes some sort of sense to her as if deep down she knew it to be true. Clearly, it doesn't make sense; I mean it's impossible to believe such things, so Jessica thought to herself. So why does she believe Christian? Why is the fear and terror leaving her body? Instead of running for the hills, committing Christian to Bellevue, she feels calm. "Jessica, I know this must all sound crazy, but . . ." Jessica places her finger gently against Christian's lips; her soft and loving smile has a way of easing Christian in the worst of moods.

"I believe you, Christian. I honestly don't know why or how, but I just do." Just as night faded in the distance, so did the fear. The two lovers were at peace with each other. As extraordinary as this all was, Jessica cared only for Christian, and he for her. Jessica furthers her understanding by meeting and talking with the Creed. She soon had a wealth of knowledge and a grasp on the situation. Although her faith was strong, doubt and fear surrounded Christian's heart. Rather than run, Jessica pledged to stand by his side throughout whatever may come. Sneaking away for a few moments, Christian stood above the rooftop of the old majestic cathedral. The city seemed some stunning; the Christmas lights gave it a warming glow. The storm was still drumming the city. Christian took a deep breath, his lounges filled with the cold night air.

Upon exhaling, a cloud of warm smoke pours out in front of him. The faint sound of thunder cracking is heard behind him. It is the Archangel Michael; he stands before Christian. His body is covered in angelic armor; the bright glow eliminates the rooftop. Christian smiles. "I had a feeling you would come. I wasn't sure if you would hear me." Michael lowers the hood from his face; a smirk of equal gesture is across his face. "I had hoped you would come around; defeating my brother is no easy task, but it is your destiny. Then again, I should have known the one person to convince you would be her." "Enough with destiny and riddles. I'm a normal twenty-one-year-old. Take me straight. How do I command these powers and kick his ass," replies Christian.

"First off, do not underestimate him; he's more connected to you then you think. Second, your powers have always been deep inside you; it's a matter of becoming one with your inner energy then merging that energy with the forces around you. See, every living thing like you is connected by energy. Our powers as angels and your powers are of the same force. It is a matter of training that inner strength with the forces around you." Michael continues to explain to Christian the depths of his powers. The two spend the entire night training. They may only be sharing a small amount of time together, but a strong bond is forming between them. "Take forming an energy blast to attack your opponent with or flying." Christian jumps on that last word. "*Flying! I* can fly?" Michael smiles in acknowledgment.

A swirl of sparkling red and blue energy circle in Michael's hand, the two colors funnel together to form a glowing ball of energy. Michael extends his arm, blasting a straight ray of energy at Christian. "Now block my attack quickly, summon energy to your arm, and strike my blast like a ball to a bat, Christian!" Christian has only seconds; trying to listen to Michael, he focuses on his arm, trying to imagine energy following into it. The air becomes still, and the city around him moves in a slow motion. Everything has become still. A rush travels through his arm.

The beam of energy hits Christian's palm rather than blast away his hand. His palm acted like a catcher mitt. In on quick motion, Christian tosses the blast away. Like now throwing the ball, he caught back at Michael. However, instead of directing it at him, the blast curves into the night sky exploding. Amazed at what just happened and how he just reflected that, he continues to train with Michael. Michael tried to make him understand that all living things have power. This force inside him and around him is the driving force behind his power. If he is to truly master the abilities inside him, he is to be connected to the universe.

"You must break the wall in your mind, the wall that tells you all this is fantasy; you must believe. Believe in yourself, tap deep into that. The power is there; use your emotions and thoughts to help that." Christian allows himself a moment to absorb what Michael said. He tries to clear his mind and break every thought of disbelief. It's not easy to believe everything that you once thought to be fiction, now reality. The two spend the bulk of the night mediating. Michael teaches him how important it is to center him, finally becoming in touch with his energy, and the energy around him. The meditation is similar to that of Buddhist teachings. Christian sits down deeply breathing; Michael teaches him to use massive concentration and awareness to fully mediate.

"Through this, Christian, you will learn you're able to sense so much around you. You can sense people—more importantly, danger. You not only can sense danger but sense dark forces, individual creates themselves. Even visions of danger to come are part of your abilities. Meditation will not only bring these powers forth but train you on using them more freely." Christian has fully emerged himself into the training with Michael. A simple rooftop conversation has turned into an educational and instructive training session.

Christian continues to mediate and practice focusing his energy. Michael fires more energy blasts at him. Christian dodges the blasts or deflects them. Calling forth energy of his own is difficult and still new to him. However, he is amazed on the power he has called forth in the short time with Michael. He has been able to increase his strength and agility greatly. His general senses are greatly heightened.

The next couple of days seem to blur together. Father Ezio discusses the location of a secret cabin outside the city. The cabin is located in a small town upstate New York in Hudson Valley. The cabin would provide an excellent location to hide out and focus on Christian's training. The cabin has been blessed, shielded from the eyes of dark creatures. If it would block Lucifer's vision or not is too been seen, no pun intended. The days are focused in training with Anthony and nights with Michael. Anthony has a different approach than Michael. Anthony doesn't really understand nor know how to teach Christian about commanding his energy or elements but rather his fighting ability, teaching him sword play and mortal combat.

Anthony strikes at Christian with a blow to his right side. His left fist collides with the side of Christian's body. Stumbling to the ground, Christian quickly reacts by dodging the following attack. Dodging the kick, Christian flips high off the ground; his flip clearly launches him twenty feet in the air. Landing back down, Christian strikes back with a ballet of attacks. Anthony struggles to block the many moves; Christian is striking at a superhuman-like speed. His hands begin to blur for Anthony. He can no longer dodge the strikes. Finally, Christian smashes his right fist across Anthony's face. The sheer force sends him flying ten feet across the open woods smashing into a tree.

The cabin is facing a massive and beautiful lake; the surrounding area is nothing but acres of forestry, a perfect area for training. In the last week, Michael and Anthony have been able to bring out moments, not consistent, but provoke some surfacing of his powers. Anthony stumbles to his feet. This was an example of provoking his powers; his strike released a massive amount of force. The problem is it's more of a bodily reaction than Christian controlling and commanding it. Anthony is trying to get him to control his inner powers by gaining more experience and knowledge on different martial art forms. Stumbling to his feet, Anthony unsheathes his sword, sprinting toward Christian. Christian, unlike Anthony, does not have a special sword blessed and given to him by the Archangel Michael. At the start of their training, Anthony gave him a blade.

Christian can feel the ground rumble underneath him as Anthony pounds his feet. The sound of the wind is cutting across his blade; it's as if his senses are so well tuned to his approaching attack. Anthony strikes the sword; Christian blocks the strike. The two swords collide, making a loud sound that echoes through the forest. The two engage in sword play, pairing with each other. Christian's form has improved greatly over such a short amount of time. He can now see the attacks as if slowing down Anthony's attacks. As they fight, Anthony is instructing him, teaching him to watch his weak points. "Guard your left side," he tells him, "keep that area covered and don't let your arm hang too much." "Keep your strikes centered. Strike the center of the blade with force, and try to strike the hilt disarming the sword. The hilt can knock the sword out of your opponent's hands."

Finishing the day of training, Christian staggers into his bedroom. The cabin is beautiful, a traditional log cabin; wood is burning in the fireplace, warming the house. The Creed has set up a whole computer terminal in the living room. Christian can hear Jessica showering inside the bathroom. The sight of steamy water seeps out of the cracks of the door and into the bedroom. Christian slowly creeps into the bathroom; Jessica is singing to herself. Christian sneaks into the shower, wrapping his arms around her. Jessica jumps; she's so startled but excited to see Christian. The two embrace each other, passionately kissing. Without Jessica's support and faith, Christian doubts he would have been to do any of this.

Christian softly lays Jessica on the bed; he kisses her body from head to toe. The overwhelming passion consumes the two of them as they consummate their love. Manhattan is cold and sinister tonight. Lucifer is hunched over an angelic statue depicting, well, him. The wind swirls loudly howling; the snow just continues to blanket massive metropolis. The sound of crackling thunder rattles the night sky; the sound reveals Mephistopheles, Aerial, and Azazel.

They bowed before him, summoned to the roof by his mind. "The time grows near; the walls that once separated this world from mine will be no more, and my legions will rise!" "And what of the prophet, my lord," replies Mephistopheles. Lucifer takes his two front fingers pressing them into his mouth, releasing such a loud whistle. The building rumbles, and the windows shutter to pieces. Imagine an entire football stadium full of people whistling together like a training choir and multiply that by ten. "I will tend to the boy; if the hounds fail, then you three will have your chance, now go." With the last of his words, the three angels disappear in a flash of light.

A faint sound can be heard in the distance—snarling and heavy panting. The sounds grow near; the pavement begins to rattle beneath him. Animal noises scare the people on the street. Unsure of what they are seeing, people shriek in terror running for cover. The two beastly hell hounds claw into the Churches side, climbing up the side to the roof. The two beasts are massive in size; their body mirrors that of a wolf, but their size is triple that of a wolf. The creature's hair and skin are jet black; its teeth are razor sharp with two sharpened fangs pointing of the sides. Giant circular eyes fill its face as red as blood.

The two hell hounds stop before Lucifer; they sit at perfect attention like a well-trained K-9. "Good boys. I believe it's time we put an end to this. Kill them all except for the boy. Do what you will to him, but bring him to me alive!" Lucifer rubs behind their ears as they moan in pleasure. He pets them on the forehead; they turn around racing for the edge of the rooftop. Howling into the night sky, they leap in a flash from rooftop to rooftop, gaining speed. "Let's see how you do against my hounds, Christian. I can feel your power growing. You're coming along. Good. Keep training. I want a real challenge."

Christian awakes next to Jessica; the two are lying in bed. Christian feels uneasy as if something forced him to wake. He can sense something coming, feeling a dark energy growing near. The hounds race toward the cabin, snarling through the woods, ripping across rows of trees. The Creed is all asleep around the fire while Markious keeps a watch. Anthony awakes, looking over at Markious; he awakes the others. They all share concerned looks hearing the sounds of trees exploding in the distant.

Jessica struggles to open her eyes, but even she can't ignore the sounds. "Baby, what is that?" Christian springs out of bed. He closes his eyes. Trying to remember what Michael said in his training, to focus his mind and meditate on the energy he feels. He can see images forming in his mind like a video struggling to load on the internet.

He can see the hounds ripping across the forest, smashing tree after tree. "Something really nasty is coming this way, and fast!" Christian grabs Jessica, running to the living room, alerting Anthony, and informing the others of his vision. It's clear the hounds are getting closer; the sounds are growing in intensity. Anthony responds to Christian, "Sounds like hell hounds." "I know I'm going to regret this, but tell me about hell hounds," replies Christian.

Anthony paints a very grim picture of the creatures. The tale sends shivers down Christian's spine and adds a level of chill in the air. The hounds are legendary in all forms of folk law; they appear in all types of mythology. One overwhelming theme was consistent that they are unstoppable killing machines. Jessica interrupted the story by asking a very direct and yet sarcastic question. "So two unstoppable killing machines are headed this way?" "I'm afraid so. They're unbelievable, hard to kill. We encountered one back during the Revolution—nasty mess that was." Jessica and Christian both look bewildered. Christian asks, "Did you just say the Revolution as in American?" Markious jumps down from the window sill. "Hate to break up this history lesson, but they're here."

Anthony grabs hold of his sword. Markious and the others do the same. "Ezio, Jessica, stay in the basement for your safety. Everybody, be on point out there; we're not dealing with some household demon or spirit but hell hounds fresh from the deep!" Christian nods to Ezio and Jessica, kissing her as if he might not kiss her again. "I love you. Whatever you do, keep this locked and stay with Ezio." Jessica makes Christian promise that no matter what, he will return to her. The two exchange another kiss. "I love you."

Outside, the snow is falling so heavily. It clouds their vision, but Christian doesn't need to see traditionally.

He uses his training to focus his mind on the area around him. His senses become more heightened, and he can feel the hounds approaching. In a blinding flash, the first hound leaps out of the forest directly for Christian. The Creed are blinded by the snow and do not notice the hound until it's too late. Christian, however, senses the creature's approach, and dodges to the side, avoiding the hound's attack. The creature smashes its head into the ground, tumbling over, flipping back to its feet. The second hound has already engaged the Creed.

Anthony slices at the beast's face; its sharp teeth knock the blade back. Markious takes aim from a distance and lunches two arrows at the beast. The arrows are pointed with an explosive head, a chemical compound similar to napalm. As it makes contact with the creature, it sends a stream of burning fire across its left side. The hound bellows out a monstrous roar, but it seems unaffected by the fire. Before Markious can launch another arrow, the hound swipes his mammoth paw, swatting him into a tree. Joseph slides across the snow and underneath his stout belly, smashing him with his staff. The creature jumps up, kicking Joseph across the ground. He goes sailing into the side of the cabin, ripping through wall.

Christopher leaps off the side of a tree, soaring above the hound, slicing his sais across the hound's forehand. The two sais cut into his forehand, pouring blood into the air. The creature's tail grabs Christopher by the neck, smashing him into the ground. Christopher loses grip of his sais, tossing them into the air.

Christian flips over the hound, dodging its tackle. Christian lands behind the creature. As of now, Christian has done a good job annoying the beast by dodging its attacks. The beast roars in anger, slashing its paw at Christian. The assault hits Christian dead center in the chest, sending him crashing to the ground. The beast leaps at him, trying to bite him in half. His enormous teeth claw at Christian. The beast seems to have the leverage over him; looking over at the Creed, he can see the other hound overpowering them as well. Christian realizes how impossible this has become. How could he think he could have done this, be a hero, command some fictional magical powers? "I'm sorry, Jess."

The hound goes to rip him in two when a blast of energy hits the side of its body, sending the creature flying into several trees. The other hound snaps in attention, looking over when it launches toward the mysterious figure. The hound slashes at the figure, but the man blocks its massive paw with his right arm. The sheer force rumbles the snow underneath them. The figure smashes the creature with his right leg; the force of the hit releases a loud crackle into the air. The hell hound moans in pain, flying across the snow.

The figure walks toward Christian. Christian is shocked. "Michael!" The mysterious figure is revealed to be the Archangel Michael. "Michael, what are you doing here? Not that I'm not grateful. I was about to be dog food." Michael helps Christian to his feet. "That won't stop them for long. You're stronger than this, Christian, remember your training, use the energy around you and inside you. I cannot stay and help you. I must attend to something else. Listen to me, all you need to do is believe, find that place in your heart, and use it." Before Christian can say anything, Michael is gone.

Christian hears faintly in the air. "Just believe, Christian, that's all you need." The other hound is already back to its feet, attacking the Creed. Anthony uses his blade to block the creature's claws. His blade sparks from the contact. He slices left and right, battling with the creature blocking his attacks. Markious jumps onto the hound's back, stabbing it with his dragger. Christopher and Joseph both slide to the back of the creature and slash his back legs. The hound groans in pain, dropping to the ground. The hound aggressively spins his paw, smacking Christopher and Joseph into the air. While spinning, Markious flies off his back and smashes into Anthony. The hound smacks them both with his snout.

Christian focuses his thoughts on something deep inside, a place in his heart where he truly believes. He tries to command the energy inside of him. The hound races toward him. He begins to form a swirling of energy in his palm; it looks like sparkling dust swirling together in his right hand. Christian continues to focus his mind on the energy. "I believe Michael. I can feel it inside of me. I have faith, please help me. If you can hear me, God, I've been a screwup—my whole life, but you choose me. Granted, I didn't exactly jump at all this, and I don't think I was the ideal candidate, but you did choose me. So please help me now. Let me believe; let me become the hero you need. I want to break free and take hold of my powers. Help me!"

With those final words, Christian forms a massive glowing ball of energy in his hand. He extends his hand forward, and a massive beam of energy rockets toward the beast. The beam cuts through the snow, melting everything around it, engulfing the beast. The hound cannot avoid the blast and is blown away into a fine dust. Christian is amazed by what just happened, but his joy is quickly interrupted when he realizes the Creed is in need of aid.

Christian runs toward them when his body lifts into the air, and he begins to fly. "Holy shit! I'm flying! Hell yea, I'm flying!" He remembers what Michael taught him about flying, thinking back on his training.

"Flying is part of your powers; think of it as defying gravity as well as space and time. You can transport in a single thought to different places and fly at great speeds. Think of your energy lifting you, think of it pushing you, and as you form energy, increasing its intensity. Think of it increasing your force forward, in turn, increasing your speed." Christian remembers these words; he can see himself lifting off the ground, hovering in front of Michael. Remembering this part of his training reminds him to command his energy, increasing his speed. He flies faster toward the Creed. Anthony and Markious are blocking its slashes. Christopher and Joseph are wounded, passed out on the ground.

Markious is cut across his side. Anthony side steps to his aid, blocking the creatures paw from smashing Markious head. Christian lands right on top of the hound's head, smashing his face into the ground. Anthony is pretty shocked. "Flying now?" Christian smiles. "You weren't the only one training me." The hound lifts up, slicing his right paw at Christian. Christian dodges to the right, sliding underneath the beast. He smashes his right elbow into the hound's stomach; the force of the blow flips it into the air on its back. Christian leaps into the air and gathers energy above his head. Christian releases a massive beam at the creature. The hound screams in pain as the blast engulfs its body. Once again, a fine dust is released into the air. Christian flies down.

"You've gained an extraordinary control over your powers, Christian." "I have to be honest, Anthony; Michael has been for these past few weeks helping my training secretly at night. Both of you have helped me to understand and gain an understanding and control. I'm very grateful, but I realized today that it came down to truly believing, committing to myself."

CHAPTER 4

BROTHERS' REUNION

Lucifer is walking through the many rows of the vast church. The cathedral is enormous; the altar is decorated with gothic statues of the Archangel Michael and Gabriel on each corner. Hanging in the middle is a crucifix; underneath is a gold-plated altar and made of limestone. The rows are polished and stained in a beautiful mahogany wood. Lucifer walks toward the altar; he pauses for a moment and stares deeply at the crucifix. "You should have listened to me back in the desert; I knew it would come to this. You can't expect these monkeys to understand what you were trying to teach them. Instead of embracing you, they crucified you. It was a testimony to their true nature; they will always live in a sin. Eventually, their greed and lust for power would have destroyed them. Your father will love me again; I will earn his trust once again."

Outside of the church, Michael crouched above the ledge. A faint crackle is heard, and appearing before Michael in a flash of light is the Archangel Gabriel. Gabriel resembles Michael and Lucifer, same angelic tunic and glowing silver armor. His face looks young and pale, with blue eyes and dirty blonde hair. "Why are you here, Michael? This is madness!" Michael rises to his feet; his stare gazes into Gabriel. The two share a moment. "You knew it would come to this. I have to confront him." Gabriel is clearly aggravated by this statement. "Why, why do you need to confront him? Your time passed its Christian's destiny now. Michael, he'll kill you."

Michael gazes upon the city lights; the sounds of the holiday cheer warm his heart. The snow storm is still fiercely attacking the city. "I know I won't make it; it's not about that. Christian is the one, Gabriel, I know that." "Then why Michael?" The sound of thunder crackling is heard in the distant, and a bright flash of light emulates the church. Michael directs his attention to the light. "The fallen are here and no doubt headed to Christian. Gabriel, we were the first; he's my brother, and I love him as one should. I will never give up one him, but you must go. Christian and the Creed will need help in the finally battle. I command you to rally our forces; the Earth will need our help." Gabriel grabs hold of Michael. The two aged and beloved friends bid farewell.

Mephistopheles, Aerial, and Azazel are speaking with Lucifer. "It seems the hounds failed at their mission. Our young hero is coming into his own. The ceremony must begin midnight, for it will be the twenty-first. I must not be disturbed during this process. Kill those fucking Creed monkeys, and bring me the boy!" Mephistopheles, Aerial, and Azazel disappeared with that final command. "I can sense you, dear brother." Michael reveals himself; the two figures stand across from each other. They look like two cowboys on high noon. "I suppose this won't make a difference, but you do not need to this, brother. Admit your sin and surround your wings to me. That is all he has ever wanted from you." Lucifer is enraged by his brother's proposal. "How dare you suggest such a thing to me, Michael, surround my wings, and fall to this plain. *I was his true son, and I will reclaim my honor!*" His words and pure aggression rattle the very foundation of the church.

"Reclaim your honor by what, brother? Destroying mankind? Do you not understand that father loves them? He always has; it's part of the plan. It's about their will; it is their will that allows them to sin but ask for love and forgiveness. You never understood that; this is not the way, and not what he wants." Lucifer draws his blade from his sheath; the blade is majestic in its design. The battle is massive and medieval in its design. The blade is two tones with a gold and silver finish. The blade is glowing brightly, emulating the area around it.

"I do not wish to fight you, brother. No matter what you've done, I still love you. I wish you could trust me and stand with me." Lucifer twirls his sword; the sword spins so quickly the brightness makes it look like a floating star. "My dear brother, you turned on me during the war and struck me down to that endless prison, for that, I will never forgive. It always was meant to come to this. When the humans are destroyed, and I free this universe of all sin, he will understand and be grateful."

Michael nods his head, unsheathing his sword. The blade is similar, but it is only a solid silver blade glowing. Lucifer slashes the blade at Michael, blocking the strike. The two blades collide, causing a wave of energy to ripple across the church. The wave rips through a handful of benches exploding them into pieces. The two go blow for blow, each delivering a thunderous sound that echoes through the streets of Manhattan. People outside hear the rumbles coming from the cathedral. The explosive energy released from their blows cuts through the church and causes damage to the city around it. People are in a panic, running for their lives and calling out for help.

Michael and Lucifer continue to battle fiercely. "I think the warm-up is over, Michael!" Lucifer leaps into the air, gripping his fists tightly; he lifts his arms above his head in the shape of an X. He screams aloud, releasing energy as his body begins to glow bright red. He releases his arms as if releasing an explosion of energy into the air. His screech complaints the explosion of energy, and his back sprouts two angelic wings. Not the traditional wings, they're not full of feathers like that of a bird but glowing streams of bright white and blue energy.

Michael also leaps into the air and releases a similar explosion of power. His body is covered in a similar glowing blue energy; his screech unleashes the same glowing wings. Both of their explosive energies destroy the walls and ground of the cathedral around them, forming a massive crater where the church once stood.

They both fly high into the sky away from the public eye and into the night, high above the clouds. Lucifer slices his sword to the left; the blade releases a slice of energy racing toward Michael. Trying to avoid the strike, Michael quickly slides to the right. The slice cuts across the sky; Michael returns the attack. The same slice of energy releases from his blade, rocketing toward Lucifer. Lucifer does not move out of the way but instead catches the slice by smacking his two hands together, grabbing it like some sort of Frisbee. Pushing his two hands together, he squashes the energy into dust, tossing it away.

Michael flies toward him, slicing his blade at the side of his head. Lucifer quickly leaps back and blocks the strike. Sparks fly from the two blades.

The two continue to deliver strike after strike, both blocking each offensive blow. "Not bad, brother, but you've grown weak these past centuries. Your power dwindles." Michael is antagonized by these words. He fires a cluster of energy beams at Lucifer. The cluster of energy soars toward him; he extends his right hand out. Each beam smashes into his hand, exploding but inflicting no damage.

Michael continues to unload his aggression by forming more energy beams, launching one after another at Lucifer. Lucifer laughs at his attempts; he smacks each blast away like swatting a bug. "Is that the best you've got, Michael?" People below can see the clouds glow brightly from their battle. Emergency vehicles have closed off the church trying to figure out what happened. Lucifer forms a massive ball of energy in his left hand and releases a colossal blast of energy at Michael. Michael widens his eyes in fear, realizing the blast is too large to dodge. He channels energy through his sword; the blade begins to glow brighter and brighter. As the beam approaches, Michael bellows loudly and slices his blade across the blast. The blade cuts through the blast, but unfortunately, it's not strong enough to cut through all of it. About halfway through, the sword gives out, and the beam knocks the sword out of his hand. The remaining blast smashes into Michael's chest, cutting deep into him. He falls back in pain, spilling blood into the air.

Michael plummets to the ground with blood streaming out of his chest. He smashes into the crater where the church once stood. Impaling into the ground at such force, an explosion of debris engulfs the area. A cloud of debris and smoke covers a handful of the surrounding blocks. Michael lies in the center of the crater moaning in pain, trying to gather strength to get to his feet. Before he can move, Lucifer smashes onto of him. The force of his land sends a ripple through the ground; blocks of concrete crack and flies into the air. Michael moans in pain, spitting blood out of his mouth.

Lucifer grabs Michael by the neck, lifting him up. "You're so pathetic to think I once fell to your hands. We could have ruled this together, brother, and instead, you choose them." Lucifer stabbed his sword through Michael. Michael fell forward onto Lucifer's shoulder, spitting more rivers of blood from his mouth. "I still love you, brother, and I always will." Sliding his sword out of him, Michael falls to the ground, taking his final breath. Lucifer stands before his fallen brother, blood dripping from his blade. You would think it to be a proud moment for him, but rather than joy, he's overwhelmed with sadness. A tear runs down the side of his cheek, and in that moment, he disappears. Emergency workers run over to the crater.

CHAPTER 5

ARMAGEDDON

Christian is strike with a sharp feeling of pain. He feels that something has happened to Michael. Christian falls to his knees, gripping his chest in pain. His mind flashes vision of Lucifer and Michael battling in the city. The images flashes quickly in his mind like strobes at a night club. The feelings and images are overwhelming. Jessica grabs hold of him. Anthony smacks his face, trying to knock him out of it. "Christian, what's wrong? Can you hear me?" Christian shacks his head coming back to reality. "It's okay. I'm okay. Something happened to Michael in the city. I think he might have been killed by Lucifer, and the fallen are headed for us." "It's a distraction, Christian. I'm sure midnight marks the twenty-first. Lucifer is preparing for the ceremony." "Anthony, I think it's time you explain to me what this ceremony entails."

"As of midnight, marking the twenty-first the planets in our solar system will form a solstice alignment. This alignment will give Lucifer the power to break free the walls that separate hell from our world. He will use this to release his full army on Earth. I don't mean the type of demons you encountered earlier. I mean pure monsters from the depths of hell, beast you can't imagine."

A blast of energy rips through the cabin. Christian grabs Jessica, tackling her to the floor. The blast passes over them, blasting through the back of the house. The front of the cabin has now been for the lack of a better word redecorated. A huge hole now presents a new opening to the cabin. Mephistopheles fires a beam of energy at Christian. Christian lunches Jessica into the air at Markious. Markious leaps up, catching her in his arms. The beam of energy smashes directly into Christian's chest, sending him crashing through the back of the cabin and tumbling into the snow.

Aerial and Azazel engage the Creed. Anthony unsheathes his sword, blocking Azazel's blade. Aerial grabs hold of Markious who handed Jessica over to Ezio. Ezio and Jessica seek cover from the battle. Aerial grabs Markious by the throat, smashing his back against a nearby tree. The trees' bark cracks, and Markious groans in pain. Aerial smashes her sword above Markious's head, and the two passionately kiss each other. "I thought you turned on me more importantly. What are you doing here, Aerial? I told you to stay away." "I told you Lucifer would have killed me if he suspected anything, and me not showing up as one of his loyal servants would have been suspicious. Rather than run now, I decided to come clean here and fight alongside you. I love you, Markious, and I don't care if I did. I'm down living a lie." Joseph and Christopher are shocked and speechless.

Joseph can't help but asks, "Markious, what's going on?" Before he can answer, they notice Anthony is being overpowered by Azazel. His sword grows weak, and Azazel is firing blast of energy at Anthony. Anthony is using his agility to dodge the blasts, but the blasts are getting more intense. Markious grabs hold of his dragger and leaps into battle, slicing at Azazel, forcing him to stop firing blasts at Anthony and sword play with Markious. Blocking his attack, the dragger and sword smash together, sending sparks into the air. The angelic sword, however, is damaging their weapons as powerful as they are. The angelic blade is stronger.

Markious falls to his knees and slices the dragger across his Azazel right knee. Grunting from the pain, Azazel smashes his leg across Markious's face. The blow rockets Markious through a nearby tree. Christopher slices his sais at Azazel; he blocks the strikes with his sword. Azazel charges energy through his sword; the connection of the sais sends the energy into Christopher. The energy shocks Christopher. Azazel then fires a small blast of energy which blasts Christopher into the air and landing hard into the ground.

Joseph smashes his staff against Azazel's back, stumbling forward the blow did minimum damage. Azazel slices his sword at the staff, cutting a chunk of its magically wood off. Azazel then kicks Joseph in the center of his chest, sending him flying across the snow. Anthony slices his sword across Azazel's face, cutting his left cheek. He then quickly spins around round house, kicking him across his face. The wound provided a good point for a quick follow up attack. Azazel drops his blade and falls to the ground. Anthony goes to cut his head off when Azazel launches a blast of energy that cuts the side of Anthony's arm.

Grabbing his arm in pain while blood oozes through his finger tips, Azazel grabs his sword, about to cut Anthony. When a blast of energy blows Azazel right away, the blast engulfs his entire right arm, blowing it away.

Christian has his hands full with Mephistopheles. The two are engaged in combat high above the ground. The two are flying above the cabin, sparring with each other. They exchange blow, blocking each other's punches and kicks. The sounds of their blows rumble the ground underneath them like a heard of buffalo. Christian smashes his fist across Mephistopheles's face. The sound of thunder is heard with each blow. Mephistopheles returns by smashing his knee across Christian's chin and combing his two hands together, smashing them downward against his back. The blow sends Christian rocketing to the ground, smashing him into a mountain of snow.

Mephistopheles flies toward him when Christian quickly recovers and launches a powerful blast of energy. The blast of energy rips through the snow and soars straight at Mephistopheles. Unaware of the attack until it's too late, the beam of energy smashed right into Mephistopheles. The exploding impact sent him tumbling into a row of trees. His body acted like a bowling ball knocking down a row of pins.

Azazel and Aerial are engaged in battle. The question is why has Aerial kissed Markious, and why has she turned against the other fallen. It's clear she has some sort of connection to Markious, but what does any of this mean? These questions fold the minds of the Creed. Azazel slices Aerial's sword out of her hand with a quick jab. This provides him with an opening, capsizing on that moment he smashes his right fist across her face. The impact of the punch releases a chilling rumble in the night sky. Aerial is hurt from the impact; her body is plummeting to the ground. Sparkling energy swirls in the palm of his hand, forming together unleashing a blast of blue and white energy. The blast hits Aerial as she smashes into the ground. The blast engulfs not only her body but the ground underneath her. Markious reacts to this by yelling out for her, but it's too late; the ground explodes as if a tomahawk missile hit it. A cloud of fire and smoke surrounds the area.

Mephistopheles flies toward Christian, releasing a horde of energy blasts at him. Christian is flying through the woods, banking through and around trees, avoiding the exploding blasts. The blasts are leveling the forest; a huge swarm of fire engulfs the arcs around them. Mephistopheles continues to unleash blast after blast; Christian continues to dodge the attacks. As he banks through another tree, he lifts his body up, climbing high above into the sky. Mephistopheles realizes he's trying to escape. "Running away, you crowd? It won't be that easy!" Flying after him, Mephistopheles doesn't know it's a trick. Christian flies through a cloud, and for a brief moment, Mephistopheles can no longer see him. Not caring, he continues to rocket toward straight ahead.

Breaking through the clouds, Mephistopheles sees a massive swirl of energy surround Christian. Christian has formed a massive swarm of energy above his head; his two hands cartel the energy like a basket. "Your over confidence blinding your senses, you should have felt this energy. Good-bye, Mephistopheles!" The blast of energy soars across the sky, cutting through the clouds like a ray of light from the heavens itself.

Mephistopheles attempts to shield himself from the blast, but his energy is no match. The force field weakens and cracks apart like shattering glass. The beam of energy begins to cut into Mephistopheles. He fights against the blast, trying to break free of its energy. The power is too great, his body begins to break away, and his skin cracks apart until his body is consumed. The blast soars to the ground, exploding into the ground. An enormous explosion fills the woods; the shockwave from the explosion sends Azazel and the Creed flying. Christian has grown weak from the last few fights; his power has grown greatly, and his training has paid off. It also feels as if a wall was broken in his mind, and his powers are now naturally following. As if a level of battle instinct has been programmed in his mind.

Azazel stumbles to his feet, staring in amazement. In front of him is a newly formed crater; the gaping hole is enormous. Markious comments to Anthony, "Well, I guess Christian graduated from the minors to the big leagues." Lying in the middle of the crater is Mephistopheles's mangled body. The remainders of his corpse crack away like a stone fading away into dust. A gust of wind carries the dust through the air. Azazel is enraged. Increasing his energy, his body begins to tremble and glow brightly. The ground underneath him begins to crack apart from the force of his energy. Azazel springs into the air, soaring toward Christian.

Azazel swings his fist at Christian; he dodges the right hook. Evading the attack, Azazel fires a blast of energy from his left hand. Christian is able to not only dodge the right hook but jump back and smack the energy blast to the side. He swats it away. Azazel continues to pursue Christian. His anger is blinding his judgment and fighting style. Azazel unleashes a cluster of attacks at Christian. He delivers punch after punch and kick after kick. Christian is blocking each of his moves; the clouds are trembling from their blows. Each blow delivers a loud, thunderous sound.

Christian lands a hard punch across his face. Azazel falls back. Christian then knees Azazel in the stomach. The impact sends such force through his body, and it causes him to lean forward, gagging in pain as blood sprouts from his mouth. Christian spins around, kicking him across the neck, lunching him toward the ground. Azazel smashes into the ground, exploding snow and pieces of dirt everywhere. Aerial is amazed at how powerful Christian has become. "Markious, he's making sport of Azazel. It's amazing." Christian descends to the ground so confident and focused. He clearly has transformed into a different person. Azazel is lying in the ground, weakened and dying.

The sun rises on the morning of the twenty-first. Lucifer is perched on the top of the Empire State Building. The moment he has been patiently awaiting has finally come to pass. Every second in that prison was to wait for this moment. Lucifer has convinced himself that the Earth must be cleansed of mankind, a quote on quote failed creation by God. The only children, as far as Lucifer is concerned, are angels. The clouds begin to swirl; lighting beings to cut across the sky. For a moment, the massive blizzard that's been hammering the city has stopped.

Now replacing the snow is violent lighting. The clouds break apart, and the sky turns black. It's as if the sun disappeared. People take to the streets, but it is not just Manhattan that the darkness has fallen on, but the entire world. People all over take to the streets; massive crowds form on city streets, parks, and residential blocks. Confused about the worldwide darkness, scientist and local media scramble to report on the situation. Governments around the world advice people to stay calm. Local law enforcement and military agencies are deployed to control the crowds.

The planets in our solar system have now aligned perfectly; the alignment sends a blot of energy charging toward Earth. Blasting through our atmosphere, the ray smashes into Lucifer. The two become one, and the beam charges Lucifer. This massive and wide beam of energy is now connected to him. "The time has come. With this, I now command my armies to come forth. Let our worlds be one!" With those words, energy ripples across the sky like pressure-cracking ice. The cracks grow in size as creatures begin to pour out. The very walls that once kept our world from hell have now been opened. Armies of demons march out; creatures of all different walks. Giant beasts come forth from beneath the Earth and invade cities all over the world. The ground breaks apart as these creatures emerge. The beats are massive in size as tall as a skyscraper. They resemble the mythical Kraken.

In Greek mythology, the Kraken is known to be a massive creature that rises from the sea. Some say it was a weapon commanded by the gods used against the Titans and then later referred to as a weapon used by Poseidon to protect the seas. The Kraken means octopus in Greek, and tales describe the creature as being similar to one. However, these creatures are not octopus. Their bodies are covered in a thick stone like skin. Sharp points stick out of their backs. Its face is covered in the cracked stone like skin with no visible eyes. Its mouth extends like a lizard with rows of razor-sharp teeth. Large tentacles swim around its body. Its tentacles are like harpoons with a flat and sharp edge to the end of them. As Revelations foretells, a beast will come from the Earth, second to the beast from the sea, directing people to worship the first. Lucifer, being the first beast, his demons will not direct but force and enslave man to worship their master.

Creatures pour out of the cracks and take to the skies, soaring above people. Massive crows of people all around the world run in panic as the huge Krakens cut across cities toppling buildings. The demons flying above the towns and cities are known as Valkyries. Like the Kraken, Valkyries are associated with ancient mythology. In Norse legends, Valkyries were believed to descend on the battlefield and take the fallen warriors who died honorable in battle to the afterlife. What people didn't know was Valkyries were a bride of pure demons created by Lucifer from the souls of men who died in sinful and bloody battle. Valkyries would continue to search for new souls in the ashes of battle fields.

They resemble that of an angel; their bodies sprout feathered wings. Their faces are deformed and horrific; they bare the expression of a tortured man. They are completely dark like the color of burnt ash. The armies of Valkyries soar across through small towns and cities, smashing through buildings and chasing people running for their lives. People run for their lives, trying to escape the destruction around them. The last piece of his army invades the world, marching by foot pounding the very Earth underneath them. Minotaurs are described in Roman and Greek legends being half man and half bull. The creature is massive in size and is depicted as a powerful warrior wielding many different weapons. Like the Valkyrie or Kraken, the Minotaur is another demonic creation by Lucifer. More tortured souls turned into a half-breed, commanded to obey his evil will. As depicted in the legends, they are ten feet tall, bull-like head, a man's body, and hind legs.

The Minotaurs wield giant axes, marching through millions of streets across the world. They smash their axes across cars, through building walls, and onto people themselves. Cornering masses of people fleeing for their lives, the Minotaurs smash their axes onto of them. Killing as much as ten people in one full swing, police try to stop the armies of demons. Firing their guns at the Minotaurs, the bullets bounce of their skin, having no effect. In Chicago, a SWAT team fires high-powered assault rifles at the Minotaurs, still no effect. Continuing to engage them, the SWAT team fires a bunch of grenades. An explosive cloud swirls around them; the army of police officers wait in silence. Their bodies tense in fear, focusing on the cloud of smoke as it slowly fades in the cold wind. Emerging out of the cloud is the unaffected army of Minotaurs.

Valkyries soar above head, swooping down on the officers, unleashing a storm of fire out of their breath. The hurricane of fire consumes the police force. A few groups of officers manage to flee, but before they can escape, the army of Minotaurs crushes them. In London, Krakens are smashing through the city, demolishing building after building. Police officers are trying to protect people and get them to safety. Air Force One has touched down in a remote area, a secret bunker where the president is meeting with key members of our government and military. "So, gentlemen, I'm going to put this the best way I know how. What in the Sam hell is going on?"

General Armstrong, a key leader in the U.S. military, directs everyone's attention to a large projected screen above the conference table. "Mr. President, as you can see, these creatures, whatever they may be, is invading all across the world. These images show that a few hours ago, they emerged from the strange cracks appearing in our skies and ground." The president seems perplexed by the images. "Do we know what these cracks are, or why they're happening?"

James Robbins, the chief scientist to the White House, directs his attention to the president. "Honestly, we don't know, sir. We believe it has something to do with the alignments of the planets, but we believe we identified the different creatures. We believe there are certain similarities to the descriptions of creatures from popular folk law. The flying creatures resemble depictions of Valkyries and armies on foot to be that of a Minotaur and possibly the large ones to be Greek Krakens."

"I must be dreaming if this is the best we have, fairy tales. All I know is people are dying; I'm ordering a fall counter strike, general. Contact our allies, and let's coordinate some type of retaliation and claim back our cities!" With those words, armies are deployed around the world. Fighter jets scramble to the skies engaging the Valkyries. In Los Angeles, F-22 raptors wind around buildings, pursuing a swarm of Valkyries. They lock onto them, firing a cluster of missiles. Colliding with the demons, the missiles unleash a cloud of smoke that rips across the sky, demolishing the buildings around it.

The assault had no effect on them; emerging from the cloud of smoke, the Valkyries tear apart the fighters. Similar instances happen across the world; fighter jets, helicopters, tanks, and armed forces are all overpowered. Armies are deployed to rally against the demonic forces but are ineffective in stopping any of the creatures. Hummers race across the burning streets of Washington; buildings are burning all over the nation's capital. Fire consumes the city streets;

buildings crumble, and bodies are littered everywhere. Soldier's spin around the corners and unload fifty caliber bullets at the marching Minotaur forces. The Kraken sends its tentacles across the city, smashing through the Hummer. The tentacles grab hold of the Hummer, lifting it into the air and crushing it tightly. The Hummer folds together like a tin can. Fighter jets fire missiles at the Kraken, unaffected by the attacks. The Kraken lunches its tentacles at the jets, ripping them into pieces. The Kraken unleashes a blast of fire out of its mouth; the fire breath consumes the buildings around it. The city is demolished in one swift blaze.

CHAPTER 6

THE ANTICHRIST

The fallen have been defeated, and since Lucifer's armies have marched through the world, Markious has been explaining his relationship with Aerial. The two meet for the first time during the American Revolution. Markious was hunting a Golem. Folk law describes Golems as creatures made of entirely inanimate matter. The truth is Golems are a hideous and deformed human soul. Many legends and pop culture fiction has described them as a zombies. Zombies may not be real in the way people think, but Golems are. They are the walking dead and do feed on human skin. The revolution was a breeding ground; many battle feeds were littered with dead bodies. It was like an all-you-can-eat-human buffet. Markious first meet Aerial on the battlefield. Markious tracked the Golems to the Battle of Princeton. A hundred people were killed during that battle; Markious was cornered by an overwhelming number of Golems.

Aerial first appeared and saved Markious. Rather than thank her, the two engaged each other in combat. Dueling it out, their aggression led to a more passionate outcome them violent. This resulted in years of secret and private sexual encounters. Over the generations, Markious and Aerial meet in different historical events—French Revolution, World War I, World War II, Vietnam, and so on.

"Listen, Lucifer's army is out there. I don't mean to put light to this subject, but I don't really care who you've been screwing for lack of a better word. I can barely sense Michael's energy. I'm going to help him and more importantly, stop Lucifer!" Jessica grabs hold of Christian, looking deeply into his eyes. "I know already; there's no point in fighting with you because you would never let me go. So I'm going to say this once. I love you with all my heart, Christian. So whatever you do, make sure you come back to me. Promise me that." "I promise you, Jess, this is my destiny, right? The moment I was born for," Christian replies. "Just make sure you believe in yourself and believe in why you're doing this. As long as you have faith, you'll be fine." Christian kisses her passionately. "Christian, we're going with you. We may not be able to help with Lucifer, but if we can kill a handful of those demons, it would be worth our lives."

"Anthony, this is it. You could die out there, all of you." Aerial steps in. "I know it's not my place, but I would like to help; if this is the end, I would like to stand with all of you." Christian places his hand on Aerial's shoulder. "It's fine with me. You guys can do whatever you desire, and I'm only interested in Lucifer." Christian instructs the Creed to grab hold of him. Each of them must touch one another, connected to him like the links of a chain. A technique that Michael taught him, Christian teleports from the cabin to the crater in Manhattan where his body is lying.

Christian runs over to Michael's body. He can sense that Michael is still alive, barely holding on. Anthony says, "He's gone, Christian." "No, I can still sense his life force; it's faint but there," replies Christian. Christian places his hand on Michael's chest. A glowing energy channels through the two. Michael awakes. He is still badly wounded. Christian grabs hold of him, lifting him to his feet. "Why did you waste your energy on me, Christian?" "Because you would do the same for me. Don't thank me too much. I barely gave you any. What happened to you?" All around them, the sounds of explosions and the rolling thunder of forces battling are heard in the fading distant. The city is consumed in destruction with roaring flames and clouds of smoke climbing to the sky. "My brother and I exchanged words." Markious laughed. "Some words." "Michael, isn't my destiny to fight Lucifer? Why would you confront him?" Michael materializes his sword in the middle of his hand.

"It's hard to explain. As confused and evil as he has become, I still love him. He will always be my brother, and I will always have faith in him." As Michael finishes his words, their bodies are transported in a blink of an eye to the middle of Times Square. Christian looks around at the square. The once beautiful glowing lights and signs of the square are demolished. The famous square that once defined the city and impressed millions are now in ruins. A figure walks through the flames and toward them. A Kraken is ripping Union Square not far from them; tanks are unloading on the creature. A woman and her young daughter are hiding behind a few cars parked in front of Christian on the corner of West Forty-Seventh Street. A Minotaur is smashing its axe on top of the car. The axe tears through the car like butter. The demon unleashes a monstrous snarl. Christian quickly reacts and bolts toward the women. The axe is inches away from hitting the women and her child. The axe hits Christian's back as he hunches over and acts as a shield protecting the women.

The axe shatters; the Minotaur is confused but angered. Swinging his fists at Christian, Christian dodges the assault. Christian upper cuts the Minotaur; the force of his punch cracks the very street underneath him. A wave of energy lifts the demon into the air and catapults him into a building. The woman is so scared; she and her daughter run off. The figure has now revealed itself as Lucifer, walking through the blocks of burning flames. "I think it's time to we talk, son." Christian snaps, "What are you talking about?" "Michael hasn't been entirely honest with you. You're my son, Christian. You are the antichrist." "Michael, what is he talking about? The antichrist is evil. He's supposed to destroy the world." Michael takes a deep breath. "He speaks the truth, Christian, you are his son. I wanted to tell you, but I was ordered not to. What you have to remember is the revelation was written in many riddles. What the truth is the antichrist is a human, and being human means freewill. You have the choice like anyone. These powers are yours, and you can make that decision what to do."

"I can't believe you lied to me, Michael. Anthony, did you guys know about this?" "No, I promise you, we didn't," replies Anthony. "Christian, you're my son, haven't you noticed everything I sent your way has been ordered to capture you not to kill you. It's to bring you to me so you can know the truth and stand with me where you belong. This is our destiny!" Christian looks confused but more than anything hurt. Everyone is standing around waiting for Christian's decision. The tension builds around them. The city is engulfed in pure destruction. The Kraken smashes through the tanks with its tentacles. Armed forces are being overrun; Valkyries soar through the city, cutting through people's apartments. "You may be my father by blood, but that means nothing to me. You're a monster.

I won't allow you to continue this. Everyone deserves a chance to be free, and I will die to protect that right!" Michael walks over to Christian, handing him his sword. "Any great warrior needs a well-crafted sword. Take mine. With your power, it will be a formidable weapon." Lucifer is angry with Christian's answer; he materializes his sword. "I'm sorry you feel this way, son, you could have been a god with me. I will kill you, son, or not."

Christian commands, "Anthony, get Michael somewhere safe and help the military forces. Help as many people as you can. I know what I need to do." Anthony and the Creed fan out, and Christian lunges at Lucifer. The epic battle has become, the moment that will define the fate of the world.

CHAPTER 7

FAITH

Christian's body starts to glow bright white. The ground starts to shake. Clouds in the sky start to circle and funnel over the city. Lucifer bellows a high pitch scream. Demons, both in the air and ground, come toward them.

Lucifer and Christian stare at each other. The Creed helps a group of soldiers a few blocks away on Fifty-Forth Street and Seventh Avenue. Lucifer and Christian continue to stare at each other, saying nothing. There just staring at each other.

Anthony and Markious combined punches to knock down a large Minotaur. The demon falls back, grabbing his step and leaping forward. Markious says, "I think we made him mad."

Anthony and Markious draw their weapons and leap forward. Lucifer smiles at Christian, bolting toward him. The ground underneath him cracks apart. The two collide, causing the ground to cave in as they thrust into the air, sending a shock wave across sky. Christian flies toward Lucifer, slicing his right arm across his chest. Lucifer quickly dodges the attack, falling back as Christian dives across his chest. Lucifer, in one swift motion, grabs Christian's arm, flipping him up into the air slicing his fist downward. The impact sends Christian rocketing to the ground and smashing him into the street below. The ground breaks into pieces, causing dust to fill the air like a cloud of smoke.

The ground rattles, and Christian rockets out of the ground like a speeding bullet. Cutting through the air crashing into Lucifer's chest head first, Lucifer falls back as Christian appears behind him, kneeing him across the left side of his face. A loud crack of thunder is heard from the hit. Lucifer smashes into a building to their right. He rips across the thirteen floor of the building smashing through desks and chairs, blasting through the other side of the building. Christian appears behind him and double fists punches him across his back, bolting him to the street corner, crashing down like a tomahawk missile. Anthony runs in front of one of the soldiers, drawing his sword, racing toward a Valkyrie, and slicing away at its face. The demon blocks the attack with his sword; the two weapons collide. The two engage in battle. Anthony slices down with his sword as the sword collides with Anthony's pushing the sword down toward Anthony's right leg. Anthony pushes the sword up; the demon slices across at his head. Anthony ducks the slices and stabs his sword across the demons stomach, cutting him in two. Lucifer grabs Christian by the neck, flying along the side of a building, grinding his face across the wall. Christian moans in pain as his body grinds into the brick wall like a knife-cutting butter. "Had enough yet, son?" Lucifer pulls him out of the building. Christian's face is full of blood. Lucifer forms an energy ball in his hand, blasting Christian across the sky.

Lucifer smashes his right arm across Christian's face; he then knees him in the stomach, causing Christian to vomit blood out of his mouth. Christian falls from atop of the building, plummeting toward the street. Before he hits the ground, he stops himself in midair, forming two energy balls in each hand. Combining the two balls of energy, he unleashes a massive blast of energy toward Lucifer. The beam engulfs Lucifer and the top of the building which he was perched on. Lucifer flies out of the smoke and punches

Christian across the face, causing the air to crack around him like the sound of a jet-breaking Mach 1. Christian flips back around, punching Lucifer across his left cheek. Christian then punches him across the stomach, causing Lucifer to gasp for air. The two exchange blow for blow as the sky shakes and rumbles from there overwhelming power.

They continue to exchange blows back and forth, causing buildings to break apart from there overwhelming energy.

Lucifer falls back, opening his mouth, unleashing a dark red fire engulfing Christian. The fire engulfs Christian as he screams in pain, smashing into an apartment window. His body lies on the floor of the apartment, smoking from the fire. He looks around to see pictures of a family who once lived there. He sees in the bathroom a demon ripping apart and eating remains of those very people. Getting up, the demon turns around, roaring at him. The Minotaur runs toward him. Christian forms a bright white light out of his hand, engulfing the demon in mid run. Lucifer sees the light cover the whole apartment. The Creed stops to see the bright light as well. As the light clears, Christian emerges, looking directly at Lucifer.

Christian and Lucifer collide, causing an energy shock rocketing across the city. Lucifer materializes his sword, lifting it above Christian's head, slicing downward.

The blade lashes out a slice that expands for miles, cutting through everything in its path. Christian quickly dodges the strike as Lucifer continues to slice over and over. Lucifer hits Christian in his arm, cutting across his shoulder. Blood spits out of Christian's shoulder, sending him crashing into a third-story window.

Rolling across a group of cubical desks, struggling to get up, Lucifer lifts his sword up as the dark clouds above him start to circle into a funnel reaching down and covering the sword. Jessica has just arrived with Father Ezio. The two made their way to the city. They hitched a ride with a military convoy. Lucifer slices the sword down, unleashing a massive blast.

Michael leaps over to try to use the last of his powers to protect everyone from the massive blast unleashed by Lucifer's sword. The explosion is massive, similar to an atomic bomb leveling the city. As the smoke clears, we see Gabriel standing in front of Christian, protecting him, as well as an angel standing in front of Michael protecting him and everyone else. Lucifer is shocked. "Gabriel, what are you doing here?" "It's been long enough, Lucifer. No more sitting on the sidelines." The clouds above open as an army of angels fly out toward the city. The armies of angels engage Lucifer's demonic forces, attacking Valkyries in the sky and Minotaurs on the ground.

Gabriel heals Michael's wounds. "I'm glad you're here. Gabriel, thank you." "Let's just hope your faith in this boy wasn't misplaced." Christian pulls his sword back, flying toward Lucifer, engaging him in heated play. Matching blow for blow, the two swords continue to collide, shaking the sky, releasing powerful energy waves. Christian kicks Lucifer across the face as he jumps back. Christian sees an opening, flying quickly toward Lucifer, pulling his sword back charging it with energy. Lucifer smiles as Christian slices the blade across his chest. Lucifer disappears and reappears behind Christian, stabbing him through the stomach. Jessica grabs his chest as her heart sinks, yelling out, *"Christian, no!* Everyone is stunned in a moment of shock. "I'll give you one thing, boy. You put up a good fight, but don't ever forget I'm the father, and you're the son. I offered you greatness, and instead, you chose death!" With those words, Lucifer slides his blade out of Christian. With his last breathes, Christian plummets to the ground.

Jessica runs over to his body, cradling him tight. Tears pour from her face. She can't believe it. Nobody can believe it. His destiny was to prevent this—save mankind from Lucifer. "It can't be, Gabriel!" Anthony and the rest of the Creed look at one another, perplexed at the outcome, but it does not change the fact that even with the help of the angels, they are still being overpowered by the demonic forces. Markious tears pieces of his clothes, trying to stop some of the bleeding, but Christian is fading away fast. Christian grabs hold of Jessica's hand, looking deeply in her eyes. "I'm sorry . . ." Christian passes away; Lucifer smiles in state of satisfaction. Christian's head falls back.

Lying there dead, Anthony runs over, performing CPR. He continues to try to awake him as he starts to scream. Tears pour down his face as he pounds on his chest. Markious pushes him away; Lucifer extends his wings, forming a bright red and white light around him. He lifts his arms up into the air. Everything begins to shake as the sky and ground starts to break apart. Even the sky breaks apart like a knife tearing it open. Gabriel looks over at Michael. "I'm afraid this is the end, the moment we feared."

Christian awakes in a strange place; his body is no longer injured. Around him is a beautiful forest with a winding, natural waterfall and spring running through the forest. Christian walks over to the spring; he sees a deer drinking water. The warm sun shines down on Christian; its rays are soothing. The sound of birds chirping makes Christian feel at ease. He can see a figure walking toward him; it's hard to make out. He tries to focus on the figure. It slowly becomes clear. It's a woman, young—and beautiful-looking woman. She has wavy burnet hair and clear blue eyes. "Hello, Christian." "Who are you? And where am I?" The woman walks over to the deer, the animal instantly frighten at all. She begins to pet it gingerly. "I go by many names, but this image is the face of your mother, Annabel." Christian is amazed. "Mom?" Tears slide down Christian's face. The woman delicately touches his face, "Oh, my son, do not cry." "I know who you really are, and I failed you." "I think it would be difficult for anyone to believe in an instant that they where the savor of man. That angels and demons existed, and you're the one to command heavenly powers to defeat them. In the world today, it would have been hard for anyone to believe."

Christian knows who the woman is. She may be in the image of his mother, but he knows she is really God. Waving her hand, the water ripples and forms an image. Christian looks upon it and sees Manhattan; he can see Jessica and the Creed. "Discovering your destiny and faith is not easy. I don't expect it to be easy for anyone. But I have faith that everyone will find it in their own way. I have sent many prophets to the world, in hopes of spreading my teachings to help people. Help guide you through the journey of life." The water underneath them starts to show images of the world throughout time. "Life isn't easy. Most of life's hardships have been created by man themselves." Christian asks, "How can you forgive us for what we've done? I mean, honestly, why don't you let Lucifer just destroy us?"

"Because I love you and always will no matter what. You never failed me, Christian. You used the gift I gave you to protect people, and you sacrificed yourself for the greater good. You didn't fail me, my son, you made me very proud."

The images show the different cities around the world and forces being overpowered by demons. The world is slowly becoming consumed. "But Lucifer won. I couldn't overpower him. I just don't have enough power; he's too strong."

"It's not about power. It was never about power. It's about faith, Christian. All I have ever asked is for people to have faith. There is no stronger power than that. You have that faith; you just couldn't see it. See it's not about faith in religion or even me. It's about faith in your life, something so powerful in your life and so real."

Christian begins to think. The images in the water turn to him and Jessica. He sees the many moments they spent together as if his fondest memories of the two were running through his mind and projecting out. "You mean, Jessica, faith in our love." "There is no greater faith or gift then that. It's the proudest thing I gave you; evil cannot and will not ever defeat good. Just channel that, and the power will be come. Always remember the light will always shine through the darkness. Be true to one another always, my son. I will be here for you whenever you need. I'm always listening, just close your eyes and pray. Spread my word, Christian. Use your powers to protect the weak and those who cannot protect themselves."

A burst of energy channels through Christian, and he is channeled back to Manhattan were he awakes. Jessica is startled, "Oh my god, Christian, it can't be." Christian doesn't say anything. He just lunches into the sky; his force is so powerful. Ripples are sent through the ground. Lucifer is hovering in the sky when he looks down to see Christian soaring toward him. Christian materializes his sword. The blade glows brightly, and in one swift motion, Christian stabs the blade into Lucifer. Lucifer tries to block the attack, but the heavens themselves open, and a powerful burst of energy empowers Christian, and his blade rips through Lucifer. Christian grabs hold of Lucifer, a huge cloud of glowing energy covers Christian's body like a floating bubble. The energy is consuming Lucifer's body. "I forgive you, Father!" Lucifer looks into the sky. *"Father, no! No!"* The energy bubble consumes Lucifer, blasting away his body into nothing. Christian throws his arms apart, releasing the bubble of energy. A white cloud of energy blasts from within in and engulfs the entire world.

As the light fades away, Jessica sees Christian standing in front of them in the middle of Times Square. People are all around them; the city is back to normal. No demons, no dead bodies, or burning buildings. It's as if it were a bad dream. Jessica turns to Michael. "What happened?" "The blast of energy somehow cleared everything, reverting the world to a state as if nothing had happened. Incredible." Jessica runs into Christian's arms, and the two kiss passionately. "How did you do that? I thought you were dead." "I had a little help and faith." Gabriel motions to Michael that it's time to go. Michael hugs Christian. "I always believed in you, Christian. Just call on me, and I will always be there for you as a friend and ally." Michael and Gabriel disappear in a quick flash of light.

"Lucifer may be gone, but the demons he's created still remain. I intend to continue to use my powers to protect people." Anthony looks at the Creed, and they all shake their heads in agreement as if understanding what Anthony is about to say before saying it. "We intend to do the same. Our whole life has been about serving man and you. I don't think we're going to stop now." Christian smiles and shakes hands with Christian. "So what do you think, Jessica?" "As long as you don't wear tights," replies Jessica.

They all laugh in joy as the world is now saved. A feeling of accomplishment and safety comes over them. A series of moments pass by in the next year, including Jessica and Christian getting married. The Creed is dressed in formal wear; even Michael and Gabriel are attending the event. Father Ezio says, "I now pronounce you husband and wife. You may kiss the bride." The two kiss passionately as their friends and family cheer aloud in the cathedral. The city is dark; sounds of police cars race by. The Creed is leaping from rooftop to rooftop in pursuit of the cars. Christian is perched on a nearby rooftop; he pulls his hood up. He's dressed in a black tunic similar to the Creeds with a gold cross on the back. "There will always be darkness, always evil. But as long as we have faith, as long as we can hold on and find our beliefs, we will understand the most important thing that evil can never overcome good because the light will always shine through the darkness." Christian leaps off the building and soars through the city.

To be continued . . .